They grow 'em tall in the saddle in Jacobsville—
and they're the best-looking, sweetest-talking men to be
found in the entire Lone Star State. They are proud,
hardworking men of steel, and it will take the perfect
woman to melt their elusive hearts....

LOVE WITH A LONG, TALL TEXAN
Diana Palmer
brings us three more Long, Tall Texans—
Guy, Luke and Christopher—
to fall passionately in love with.

*Now meet the ladies who stake a claim on the men of
Jacobsville:*

Candy Marshall: This feisty, secretly vulnerable
publicist saw a different side to maverick cowboy
Guy Fenton. She enticed him with her soft, sweetly
tantalizing kisses—and vowed to help him turn his life
around once and for all!

Belinda Jessup: When one of her young charges
made mischief on cattleman Luke Craig's ranch, this
headstrong social worker locked horns with the fit-to-
be-tied bachelor. Would their discord give way to happily
ever after?

Della Larson: She was a sharp-witted newswoman who
embarked on an exciting adventure with life-hardened
Christopher Deverell. But when he awakened her
womanly passion, she realized she'd found the man of
her dreams....

"Diana Palmer makes a reader want to find a Texan
of her own to love!"

—*Affaire de Coeur*

Dear Reader,

I love surprises. Perhaps it's because I enjoyed reading O. Henry's stories when I was still in school. Nothing gives me more pleasure than "twist" endings and hidden clues that lead to unexpected revelations about characters, as you are probably going to notice when you read these three new LONG, TALL TEXAN short stories.

Each of these characters had a part in an earlier work. Guy Fenton and Luke Craig first appeared in *A Long Tall Texan Summer*, an earlier collection of my short stories. Christopher Deverell was a minor character in my MOST WANTED Silhouette Desire series. I've had a number of letters from readers about these guys, so now they have their own stories. You'll also notice the brief appearance of some other characters who will be familiar, too!

For those of you who have asked about the fate of Mather ("Matt") Caldwell, I am working on his book right now, a Silhouette Special Edition. And as long as Silhouette is kind enough to publish them, there definitely will be more LONG, TALL TEXAN books!

Thank you all for your kindness and support all these years. I so enjoy hearing from all of you, even if I am slow on replies!

Love,

Diana Palmer

DIANA
LOVE WITH A
LONG, TALL TEXAN
PALMER

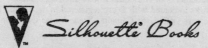

Silhouette Books

Published by Silhouette Books
America's Publisher of Contemporary Romance

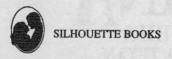

SILHOUETTE BOOKS

LOVE WITH A LONG, TALL TEXAN

Copyright © 1999 by Diana Palmer

ISBN 0-373-48379-1

GUY
Copyright © 1999 by Diana Palmer

LUKE
Copyright © 1999 by Diana Palmer

CHRISTOPHER
Copyright © 1999 by Diana Palmer

This edition published by arrangement with Harlequin Books S.A.

® and TM are trademarks of Harlequin Books S.A., used under license. Trademarks indicated with ® are registered in the United States Patent and Trademark Office, the Canadian Trade Marks Office and in other countries.

Look us up on-line at: http://www.romance.net

Printed in U.S.A.

CONTENTS

Diana Palmer is legendary for her unforgettable
tales about those long, lean, lovable
Long, Tall Texans....

Be sure to look for more LONG, TALL TEXANS
in your local stores, or contact our
Silhouette Reader Service Center,
USA.: 3010 Walden Avenue
P.O. Box 1325, Buffalo, NY 14269
Canada: P.O. Box 609, Fort Erie, Ontario L2A 5X3

THE MESMERIZING MEN
OF JACOBSVILLE, TEXAS

By Request's	
LONG,	CALHOUN BALLENGER & ABBY CLARK
TALL	JUSTIN BALLENGER & SHELBY JACOBS
TEXANS I	TYLER JACOBS & NELL REGAN
By Request's	
LONG,	QUINN SUTTON & AMANDA CALLAWAY
TALL	ETHAN HARDEMAN & ARABELLA CRAIG
TEXANS II	CONNAL TREMAYNE & PEPI MATHEWS
By Request's	
LONG,	HARDEN TREMAYNE & MIRANDA WARREN
TALL	EVAN TREMAYNE & ANNA COCHRAN
TEXANS III	DONAVAN LANGLEY & FAY YORK
By Request's	
LONG,	EMMETT DEVERELL & MELODY CARTMAN
TALL	THAT BURKE MAN—TODD BURKE & JANE PARKER
TEXANS IV	REGAN'S PRIDE—TED REGAN & COREEN TARLETON
A LONG	TOM WALKER & ELYSIA CRAIG
TALL TEXAN	DREW MORRIS & KITTY CARSON
SUMMER	JOBE DODD & SANDY REGAN

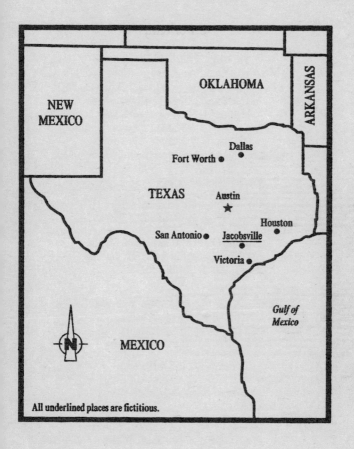

All underlined places are fictitious.

For Kim

GUY

"See! How she leans her cheek upon her hand:
O! That I were a glove upon that hand,
That I might touch that cheek."

—William Shakespeare
Romeo and Juliet, II, ii, 23

ONE

Chapter 1

It was a cool autumn day, and the feedlot was full. A good many of these steers were already under contract to restaurants and fast-food establishments, but in these last weeks before they were shipped north, the cowboys who worked for the Ballenger Brothers in Jacobsville, Texas, were pushed to the limit. Guy Fenton hated his job when things were this hectic. He almost hated it enough to go back to flying; but not quite.

He pushed his hat back from his sweaty dark hair and cursed the cattle, the feedlot, people who ate beef, and people who bought it in eloquent succession. He wasn't a handsome man, but he still had a way with women. He was lean and lanky, thirty years old, with gray eyes and a tragic past that an occasional date numbed just a little. Lately, though, women had been right off his list of pastimes. There had been too much work here at the feedlot, and he was responsible for mixing the various grains and nutrients to put just enough, but not too much, weight on these beef cattle. He enjoyed the job from time to time, but just lately everything was rubbing him the wrong way. A chance meeting with an old acquaintance several months ago from the days of his engagement had brought back all the bad memories and set him on a weekend binge. That was followed by another, when the man settled nearby and came to visit him occasionally, not realizing the damage he was doing to Guy's peace of mind.

"For two bits," he said out loud, "I'd chuck it all and become a beachcomber!"

"Keep your mind on that conveyor belt and thank God you don't have to climb down in there to inoculate those horned devils," came a drawling voice from behind him.

He glanced over his shoulder at Justin Ballenger and grinned. "You don't mean things could get worse around here?"

Justin stuck his hands into his pockets and chuckled. "It seems that way, from time to time, when we get this much extra business. Come over here. I want to talk to you."

The big boss rarely came out to talk to the hands, so it was an occasion for curiosity. Guy finished the settings on the conveyer belt that delivered feed to the dozens of stalls before he jumped down lithely to stand before one of the two owners of the feedlot.

"What can I do for you, boss?" he asked pleasantly.

"You can stop getting drunk every weekend and treeing Thompson's place," he replied solemnly, his dark eyes glittering.

Guy's high cheekbones went a little ruddy. He averted his gaze to the milling, mooing cattle. "I didn't realize the gossip got this far."

"You can't trim your toenails in Jacobsville without somebody knowing about it," Justin returned. "You've been going downhill for a while, but just lately you're on a bad path, son," he added, his deep voice quiet and con-

cerned. "I hate to see you go down it any farther."

Guy didn't look at the older man. His jaw
tautened. "It's my road. I have to walk it."

"No, you don't," Justin said curtly. "It's
been three years since you signed on here. I
never asked any questions about your past, and
I'm not doing it now. But I hate to see a good
man go right down the drain. You have to let
go of the past."

Guy's eyes met the other man's almost on a
level. Both were tall, but Justin was older and
pretty tough, too. He wasn't a man Guy would
ever like to have to fight. "I can't let go," he
replied shortly. "You don't understand."

"No, I don't, not in the way you mean,"
Justin conceded, his dark eyes narrowing.
"But all this carousing and grieving isn't go-
ing to change whatever happened to you."

Guy drew in a short breath and stared at the
flat horizon. He didn't speak, because if he let
the anger out, Justin would fire him. He might
hate his job, but he couldn't afford to lose it,
either. "Rob Hartford settled up in Victoria
and he comes down to see me. He does it too
often," he said finally. "He was there—when

it happened. He doesn't know it, but he brought all the memories back.''

"Tell him. People can't read minds.''

He sighed. His gray eyes met Justin's dark ones. "He'd take it hard.''

"He'll take it harder if you end up in jail. The one good thing about it is that you've got sense enough not to drive when you're in that condition.''

"The only good thing," Guy said wearily. "Okay, boss, I'll do what I can.''

Justin followed his gaze. "Winter's coming fast," he murmured. "We'll just get this batch of steers out before we have to buy more feed. It'll be close, at that.''

"Only crazy people get into feeding out cattle," Guy pointed out, lightening the atmosphere.

Justin smiled faintly. "So they say.''

He shrugged. "I'll try to stay away from Thompson's.''

"It doesn't make a hell of a lot of sense to drink up your salary every weekend," the older man said flatly. "Regardless of the reason. But that isn't what I came out here to talk to you about.''

Guy frowned. "Then why did you?''

"We've got a beef industry publicist coming tomorrow from Denver. She wants to visit a few area ranches as well as our feedlot here, to get some idea of what sort of methods we're using."

"Why?" Guy asked curtly.

"The local cattlemen's association—of which Evan Tremayne was just elected president—wants to help punch up the image of the industry locally. The industry as a whole has had some bad press lately over bacterial contamination. There's been even more bad press about some renegade cattlemen and their practices. We don't follow their lead around here, and we're anxious to get the fact across to the beef-eating public. Evan also has an idea about customizing lean beef for a specialized market of buyers."

"I thought Evan was too busy with his wife to worry about business," Guy murmured dryly.

"Oh, Anna's doing his paperwork for him," he mused. "They're inseparable, business or not. Anyway, this publicist is expected in the morning. The Tremaynes are out of town, Ted Regan and his wife are at a convention in Utah, and Calhoun and I are going to be tied up with a buyer tomorrow. You're the only cowboy we've got who knows as much about the industry as we do, especially where feedlots are concerned. We've elected you to be her guide.''

"Me?'' Guy cursed under his breath and glared at the older man. "What about the Hart boys? There are four of them over at the Hart ranch.''

"Two,'' Justin corrected. "Cag's off on his honeymoon, and Corrigan went with his wife, Dorie, to visit Simon and Tira in San Antonio. They've just had their first child.'' He chuckled. "Anyway, I wouldn't wish the two bachelor Hart boys on her. We don't know if she can make biscuits, but Leo and Rey may be too desperate to care.''

Guy only nodded. The Hart boys were a local legend because of their biscuit mania. Pity none of them could cook.

"So you're elected.''

"I know more about rodeo than I know about ranching,'' Guy pointed out.

"Yes, I know.'' He searched the younger man's closed face. "I heard someone say you used to fly yourself to the competitions.''

Guy's eyes glittered and he straightened. "I don't talk about flying. Ever."

"Yes, I heard that, too," Justin said. He threw up his hands. "All right, clam up and fester. I just wanted you to know that you'll be away from here tomorrow, so delegate whatever chores you need to before in the morning."

"Okay." Guy sighed. "I guess you couldn't do it, or Calhoun?"

Justin glanced over his shoulder. "Sorry. Shelby and I have to go to the elementary school in the morning. Our oldest son's in a Thanksgiving play." He grinned. "He's an ear of corn."

Guy didn't say a word. But his eyes danced and his lower lip did a tango.

"Good thing you kept your mouth shut, Fenton," he added with a wicked grin. "I hear they're shy a turkey. It would be a pity to volunteer you for *that* instead of the ranch tour."

He walked off and Guy gave in to the chuckle he'd choked back. Sometimes he didn't mind this job at all.

He went back to the bunkhouse after work, noting that it was empty except for one young college student from Billings, who was sprawled on a bunk reading Shakespeare through small rimmed glasses. He looked up when Guy entered the building.

"Cook's off sick, so they're shuttling supper out from the main house," the college student, Richard, remarked. "Just you and me tonight. The other bachelors went off to some sort of party in town."

"Lucky stiffs," Guy murmured. He took off his hat and sprawled on his own bunk with a weary sigh. "I hate cattle."

Richard, who liked to be called "Slim" by the other cowhands, chuckled. He was much more relaxed when he and Guy were the only two men sharing the bunkhouse. Some of the older hands, many uneducated, gave him a hard time in the evenings about his continuing studies.

"They may smell lousy, but they sure do pay my tuition," Slim remarked.

"How many years do you have to go?" Guy asked curiously.

The younger man shrugged. "Two, the normal way. But I have to work a semester and go to school a semester, because it's the only way I can afford tuition. I guess it'll take me four more years to graduate."

"Can't you get a scholarship?"

Slim shook his head. "My grades aren't quite good enough for the big ones, and my folks make too much money for me to qualify for financial aid."

Guy's eyes narrowed. "There should be a way. Have you talked to the finance office at your school?"

"I thought about it, but one of the other kids said I might as well save my time."

"What's your field?"

Slim grinned. "Medicine," he said. "So I've got a long road ahead of me, even after I get my B.S."

Guy didn't smile. "I've got a couple of ideas. Let me think them over."

"You've got problems of your own, Mr. Fenton," Slim told him. "No need to worry about me as well."

"What makes you think I've got problems?"

Slim closed the literature book he was holding. "You get drunk like clockwork every weekend. Nobody drinks that much for recreation, especially not a guy who's as serious the rest of the week as you are. You never shirk duties or delegate chores, and you're always stone sober on the job." He smiled sheepishly. "I guess it was something pretty bad."

Guy's pale gray eyes had a faraway, haunted look. "Yes. Pretty bad." He rolled over onto his back and pulled his hat over his eyes. "I wish you outranked me, Slim."

"Why?"

"Then you'd get stuck with the publicist tomorrow, instead of me."

"I heard Mr. Ballenger talking about her. He says she's pretty."

"He didn't tell me that."

"Maybe he was saving it for a surprise."

Guy laughed hollowly. "Some surprise. She'll probably faint when she gets a good whiff of the feedlot."

"Well, you never know." Pages in the book rustled as he turned them. "Man, I hate Shakespeare."

"Peasant," Guy murmured.

"You'd hate him, too, if you had to do a course in medieval literature."

"I did two, thanks. Made straight *A*'s."

Slim didn't speak for a little while. "You went to college?"

"Yup."

"Get your degree?"

"Yup."

"Well, what in?"

"In what," Guy corrected.

"Okay, in what?"

"You might say, in physics," he said, without mentioning that his degree was in aeronautics, his minor in chemistry.

Slim whistled. "And you're working on a cattle ranch?"

"Seemed like a good idea at the time. And it's sure physic-al," he added with a deliberate play on words.

Laughter came from across the room. "You're pulling my leg about that physics degree, aren't you?"

Guy smiled from under his hat. "Probably. Get back to work, boy. I need some rest."

"Yes, sir."

Guy lay awake long into the night, thinking about college. He'd been a lot like Slim, young and enthusiastic and full of dreams. Aviation had been the love of his life until Anita came along. Even then, she was part of the dream, because she loved airplanes, too. She encouraged him, raved over his designs, soothed him when plans didn't work out, prodded him to try again. Even when things were darkest, she wouldn't let him give up on the dream. And when it was in his grasp, she never complained about the long hours he was away from her. She was always there, waiting, like a dark-haired angel.

He'd given her the ring just before they went up together, that last time. He was always so careful, so thorough, about the plane. But that once, his mind had been on Anita instead of the engine. The tiny malfunction, caught in time, might have been rectified. But it wasn't. The plane went down into the trees and hung, precariously, in the limbs. They could have climbed down, only bruised, but Anita had fallen heavily against the passenger door and, weakened by the crash, it had come open. He saw her in his nightmares, falling, falling, forty feet straight down to the forest floor, with nothing to break the fall except hard ground, her eyes wide with horror as she cried his name—

He sat straight up on the bunk, sweating, barely able to get his breath as the nightmare brought him awake. Slim was sleeping peacefully. He wished he could. He put his head in his hands and moaned softly. Three years was long enough to grieve, Justin said. But Justin didn't know. Nobody knew, except Guy.

He was half-asleep the next morning when he went down to the feedlot in clean blue jeans and a blue-and-white checked flannel shirt under his sheepskin jacket. He wore his oldest Stetson, a beige wreck of a hat, wide-brimmed and stained from years of work. His boots didn't look much better. He was almost thirty-one years old and he felt sixty. He wondered if it showed.

Voices came from Justin's office when he walked into the waiting room at the feedlot. Fay, J. D. Langley's pretty little wife, smiled at him and motioned him on in. She was technically Calhoun Ballenger's secretary, but today she was covering both jobs in the absence of the other secretary.

Guy smiled back, tipped his hat, and walked on in. Justin stood up. So did the pretty little brunette with him. She had the largest, most vulnerable brown eyes he'd ever seen in a human being. They seemed to see right through to his heart.

"This is Candace Marshall, Guy," Justin said. "She's a freelance publicist who works primarily for the cattle industry. Candy, this is Guy Fenton. He manages the feedlot for us.''

Guy tipped his hat at her, but he didn't remove it. He didn't smile, either. Those eyes hurt him. Anita had brown eyes like that, soft and warm and loving. He could see them in his nightmares as she cried out for him to help her—

"I'm pleased to meet you, Mr. Fenton," Candy said solemnly, and held out a hand toward him.

He shook it limply and without enthusiasm, immediately imprisoning both his hands in the pockets of his jeans.

"Guy is going to show you the ranches in the area, before he familiarizes you with the feedlot itself," Justin continued. He produced two typed sheets and handed one to Guy and one to Candy. "I had Fay type these for you. There's a map on the back, in case you don't recognize where the ranches are located. The local ranches contract with us to custom-feed their yearling bulls and replacement heifers," he explained to Candy. "We do some out-of-state business, too, with consortiums like Mesa Blanco, which Fay's husband, J. D. Langley, operates. Any details you need about daily routine and operation, and costs, Guy can give you. He's been with us for three years now, and he's very good at his job. He's in charge of the feeding schedules, which are scientific in the extreme.''

Candy studied Guy with new interest. "Scientific?"

"He minored in chemistry," Justin added. "Just what we need here to work out feed concentrates and nutritive combinations, all to do with weight-gain ratios, the bottom line of which is profit."

She smiled softly at Justin, pushing back a long strand of dark hair that had escaped from the French twist at her nape. "My dad was a cattleman, so I know a bit about the business. My mom runs one of the biggest ranches in Montana, in fact."

"Does she, really?" Justin asked, impressed.

"She and J. D. Langley and the Tremayne boys gang up on the others at cattlemen's conventions," she continued. "They're radicals."

"Don't tell me," Justin groaned. "No additives, no hormones, no antibiotics, no pesticides, no herbicides, no cattle prods—"

"You *do* know J.D.!" Candy chuckled.

Guy was trying not to notice her resemblance to Anita. She was very pretty when she smiled.

"Everybody around here knows J.D.," Justin said with an exaggerated sigh. He glanced at the Rolex watch on his left wrist. "Well, I've got visiting cattlemen due, so I'll let you two get down to business."

Candy was glancing hurriedly at the list. She grimaced. "Mr. Ballenger, we can't possibly see all these ranches in one day!"

"I know. We figure it will take a week or so. We've booked you into our best motel. The cattlemen's association will pick up the tab, including meals, so don't skimp on food." He frowned, noting her extreme thinness and pallor. "Are you all right?"

She straightened and smiled with something like deliberation. "I'm just getting over a bad case of flu," she said slowly. "It's hard to pick up again."

"So it is. Early for the flu."

She nodded. "Yes, it is, isn't it?"

Justin hesitated, then shrugged. "Take it easy, just the same. Guy, if you don't mind, check in with Harry every morning and give him his instructions. I know they're pretty much cut-and-dried for the next week, but do it just the same.''

"Sure thing, boss," Guy said lazily. "Well, Miss Marshall, shall we go?"

"Of course." She started slowly toward her compact rental car when she noticed that Guy was going in the opposite direction.

"Mr....Fenton?" she called, having had to stop and remember his name.

He turned, his hands still deep in his pockets. "This way," he said. "We'll go in one of the ranch trucks. You'll never get that thing down Bill Gately's pasture without a broken axle.''

"Oh." She stared at the car and then at the big black double-cab pickup truck with the Ballenger logo in red on the door. "I see what you mean." She went toward the truck in that same, slow gait, a little winded by the time she reached it. She stepped on the running board, displaying a slender, pretty long leg as her skirt rode up. Catching hold of the handhold just above the door, she pulled herself up and into the seat with a gasp.

"You're out of condition," he murmured. "Bronchitis?"

She hesitated just a second too long before answering. "Yes. From the flu."

"I'll try to keep you out of feed dust on the tour," he said, closing the door tight behind her.

She had to sit and catch her breath before she could struggle into the seat belt. All the while, Guy Fenton sat holding the steering wheel in one gloved hand while he observed her pale complexion and flushed cheeks. She looked unwell.

"I got out of bed too soon," she said finally, pushing back a loose strand of dark hair. "I'm fine. Really." She forced a smile and her big brown eyes softened as she looked at him.

He almost groaned. Memories hit his heart and made his breath catch. He flicked the key in the ignition and put the truck in gear. "Hang on," he said tautly. "We've had a lot of rain and the roads are a mess."

"Muddy, huh?" she asked.

"Muddy. Some are washed out."

"Winter floods," she mused.

"El Niño," he informed her. "It's played havoc with the West Coast, the East Coast, and all points in between. I don't think I've seen this much rain in Texas in my lifetime."

"Were you born here?"

"I moved here three years ago," he said tersely.

"Not a native Texan, then." She nodded.

He glanced at her. "I didn't say I wasn't born in Texas. Just that I wasn't born in Jacobsville."

"Sorry."

He looked back at the road, his jaw taut. "No need to apologize."

She was pulling hard at air, as if she couldn't get enough in her lungs. She leaned her head back against the seat and closed her eyes for a minute. Her eyebrows drew together, as if she were in pain.

He put on the brakes and slowed the truck. Her eyes opened, startled.

"You're ill," he said shortly.

"I'm not," she protested. "I told you, I'm still weak from the flu. I can handle my job, Mr. Fenton. Please don't...don't concern yourself," she added stiffly. She turned her head and stared out the window at the bleak winter landscape.

He frowned as he pulled ahead down the rough track that led to the main road. She was prickly when he referred to her health and he'd have bet she was hiding something. He wished he knew what it was.

The first ranch on the agenda was owned by old Bill Gately, on the Victoria road. It wasn't the showplace of most ranches around Jacobsville, a fact which Guy pointed out to her when they arrived.

"Bill hasn't moved with the times," he told her, his eyes on the road ahead. "He grew up in the 'thirties,' when ranching was still done the old-fashioned way. He doesn't like the idea of feeding cattle anything supplemental, but when we were able to prove to him the weight-gain ratios we could get, he caved in." He glanced at her with a wry smile. "Not that he's completely sold. And he's going to have trouble with you, I'm afraid."

She chuckled. "Women don't belong in the cattle industry, I gather, and how could the cattlemen's association be blind enough to let them do publicity—and why do we need publicity, anyway, when everybody loves steak?"

"Pretty good," he said. "He'll trot out all those arguments and a few more besides. He's seventy-five and he can run circles around some of our cowboys." He glanced at her.

"We have it on good authority that he knew
Tom Mix personally and once, briefly, had
charge of grooming Tony."

"I'm impressed," she said.

"You know who Tom Mix is?"

She laughed. "Doesn't everybody? He was
as much a showman as a movie star. I have
several of his silent films, and even a talkie."
She shrugged. "I don't care a lot for most
modern films, with the exceptions of anything
John Wayne starred in."

He navigated a tricky turn and changed
gears as they went down what looked like a
wet ravine. "See what I meant about this
place?" he asked as she held on for dear life
while the truck manfully righted itself at the
bottom of the sheer drop.

"I sure do," she agreed, catching her
breath. "What does Mr. Gately drive?"

"He doesn't," he informed her. "He goes
where he has to go on horseback, and if he
needs supplies, he has them brought in." He
grinned. "The grocer in town has a four-wheel
drive, or I guess old Bill would starve."

"I should think so!"

He shifted back into high gear. "How did
your mother become a rancher?"

"My dad was one," she said simply. "When he died, she kept the place going. It was difficult at first. We had ranch hands like your Mr. Gately, who were still living in the last century. But my mother is a law unto herself, and she gathers people in without even trying. People just love her, and they'll do whatever she asks. She's not bossy or sharp, but she's stubborn when she wants her own way."

"That's surprising," he said. "Most women in positions of authority are more like overbearing generals than women."

"Have you known a lot?" she returned.

He pursed his lips and thought. "I've seen plenty in movies."

She shook her head. "Most of which are written by *men*," she pointed out. "What you get in cinema and even in television is some man's idea of a woman authority figure. I've noticed that not many of them are true to life. Certainly they aren't like my mother. She can shoot a Winchester, round up cattle, and build a fence—but you should see her in a Valentino gown and diamonds."

"I get the point."

"It's been a long road for her," she said.

"I'm sorry Dad died when he did, because she's known nothing but work and business for most of her life. It's made her hard." And as cold as ice, she could have added, but didn't.

"Any brothers or sisters?"

She shook her head. "Just me." She turned her head toward him. "How about you?"

"I have a brother. He's married and lives in California. And a married sister up in Washington State."

"You've never married?"

His face became hard as stone. He shifted the gears again as they approached the rickety old ranch house. "Never. There's Bill."

Chapter 2

Bill Gately was white-headed and walked with a limp, but he was slim and as spry as most men half his age. He shook hands politely with Candy and lifted a bushy eyebrow but made no comment when he was told what her job was.

"Justin Ballenger said that you wouldn't mind letting us look over your place," Candy said. She smiled. "I understand that you've made some amazing progress here in the area of old forage grasses."

His blue eyes lit up as if plugged into an

electrical socket. "Why, so I have, young
lady," he said enthusiastically. He took her by
one arm and led her around to the back of the
house, explaining the difficulty of planting and
cultivating such grasses. "It wouldn't be fea-
sible on a large scale because it's too expensive, but I've had great success with it and I'm
finding ways to bring down the cost with the
use of mixing common grasses with cultivated
ones. The calves forage on these grasses, on a
rest-rotation grazing system, until they're year-
lings and then I send them over to Justin and
Calhoun to have them fed out for market." He
smiled sheepishly. "I've shown some pretty
impressive weight gains, too. I should probably let the Ballengers do my marketing as well,
but I like to do my own selling, keep my hand
in. I only have about a hundred head at a time,
anyway, and that's a small lot for the brothers
to want to bother with."

"Where do you usually sell your stock?"
she asked curiously.

"To a hamburger chain," he said, and
named it. It was a local chain that had started
on a shoestring and was now branching out to
larger cities.

Her eyebrows lifted. "I'm really impressed," she said. "Most hamburger joints were buying all their beef from South America until the news about the dwindling rain forest got out. After that, a number of chain restaurants lost customers because people were upset about South American ranchers cutting down rain forest to make way for pasture for their beef cattle."

He grinned. "That's the very argument I used on them!" he told her with a sweeping gesture. "It worked, too. They're even starting to advertise their hamburgers as the ones that don't come from the rain forest, and if they wanted to, they could advertise it as 'organically grown,' because I don't use anything artificial in their diets."

She sighed. "Oh, Mr. Gately, if only we could package and sell *you!* What a marvelous approach to cattle raising."

He blushed like a young girl. Later, he got Guy to one side and told him that he'd never met anyone as capable as Candy at publicizing the cattle industry.

Guy related the story to his companion as they wound down the road toward Jacobsville.

The Gately ranch had taken up most of the afternoon, because Candy checked Bill's research journal for his progress with several other strains of old grasses, like the old buffalo grass, which had largely been destroyed on the Western plains by farmers in the early days of settlement. It had been a productive session.

"You're very thorough," Guy commented.

She was reading her notes but she looked up at his tone. "Did you expect someone slipshod to do such important work?" she asked.

He held up a lean, strong hand. "I wasn't throwing out a challenge," he told her. "I only meant that you seem pretty good at what you do."

She leaned back against the seat with a little sigh. "I take pride in my work," she confessed. "And it hasn't been an easy job from the beginning. There are plenty of cattlemen like Mr. Gately, only less easily convinced, who enjoy making me as uncomfortable as possible."

"How?"

"Oh, they make sure I'm escorted past the breeding pastures when the bulls are at work," she mused, tongue-in-cheek, "and into the

barn when the cows are being artificially in-
seminated. I once had a rancher discuss his cattle weight-gain ratios in front of a stable where
a mare was being bred. He had to shout to
make himself heard.''

He whistled. "I'm surprised. I thought most
men in this business had a little respect for the
opposite sex.''

"They do, as long as she's in a kitchen making biscuits.''

"Don't say biscuits around the Hart boys,
whatever you do!'' he exclaimed. "Rey and
Leo are still single, and I could tell you some
incredible tales about the lengths they've gone
to for a biscuit feast since Corrigan and Simon
and Cag got married and moved out of the
main house!''

She chuckled. "I've heard those all the way
back at our main office in Denver,'' she confided. "At any cattle convention, somebody's
got a story to tell about the Hart boys. They
get more outrageous by the day.''

"And more exaggerated.''

"You mean it wasn't really true that Leo
carried a cook bodily out of the Jacobsville

café one morning and wouldn't let her go until she made them a pan of biscuits?''

"Well, that one was..."

"And that Rey didn't hire one of the cooks in Houston to make him four whole trays of uncooked biscuits, which he hired a refrigerated truck to take down to the ranch for them?''

"Well, yes, he did..."

"And that when Mrs. Barkley retired from the Jones House restaurant in Victoria, Rey and Leo sent her red roses and truckloads of expensive chocolates for two weeks until she agreed to give up retirement and go work for them last month?''

"She's allergic to roses, as it happens," he murmured dryly, "and she was gaining a lot of weight on those chocolates.''

"She's probably allergic to those Hart boys by now, poor soul," she said with a tiny laugh. "Honestly, I've never been around any such people!''

"You must have characters back home in Montana.''

She dusted off her skirt. "Sure we do, but only like old Ben who used to hang out with

Kid Curry and Butch Cassidy, and served time for being a train robber,'' she replied.

He grinned at her. ''Beats stealing a cook.''

''I don't know. I understand one of the Hart boys keeps a giant snake. His poor wife!''

''He had an albino python, but when he married Tess, he gave it to a breeder. He visits Herman occasionally, but he wouldn't ask Tess to live with it.''

''That's nice.''

''Cag is a lot of things. Nice isn't one of them.'' He thought for a minute. ''Well, maybe his wife likes him.''

''No wonder his best friend was a reptile.''

''You're sounding a little winded,'' he remarked. ''That wheat straw in the corral wasn't too much for you, was it? The wind was blowing pretty hard.''

She stared at him blankly. ''Am I supposed to notice a connection between that and my being breathless?''

He lifted a shoulder. ''Why don't you use your medicine?''

She stilled. ''What medicine?''

''Surely you know you're asthmatic?''

She kept right on staring at him, her eyes

turbulent, although he couldn't see them. "I don't—have asthma," she said after a minute.

"No? You could have fooled me. You can't walk ten steps without resting. At your age, that's pretty unusual."

Her jaw clenched and her pretty hands had a stranglehold on her purse as she stared out the window.

"No comment?" he persisted.

"Nothing to say," she returned.

He would have pursued it, but they were already going down the main street in Jacobsville, barely a block from her hotel.

"My rental car," she began.

"I'll pick up Slim. He can drive it over here and ride back with me. Got the keys?"

She handed them to him warily. "I'm perfectly capable of driving. There's nothing wrong with me!"

"I'd do it for anyone," he said, acting puzzled. "You've had a long day. I thought you might be tired."

"Oh." She flushed a little as they reached the hotel and he pulled up in front of it. "I see. Well, thank you, then."

He parked the truck, got out, and went

around to help her down from the high cab. She seemed to resent that, too.

He frowned down at her. "What put that chip on your shoulder?" he asked. "You're overly sensitive about any sort of help."

"I can get out of a truck by myself," she said shortly.

He shrugged. "I do it for a great-uncle of mine," he informed her. "He's not old, but he has arthritis and appreciates a helping hand."

She flushed. "You make me sound like a militant feminist!"

His pleasant tone had been deceptive. The eyes that met hers were ice-cold and completely unfriendly. "You're about that unappealing, yes," he said bluntly. "I like a woman who can command respect without acting like a shrew or talking down to men. You don't like doors opened for you or concern for your health. Fine. I can assure you that I won't forget again." His jaw clenched. "My Anita was worth ten of you," he added roughly. "She was spirited and independent, but she never had to prove she was a man in a dress."

"Why didn't you marry her, then?"

"She died," he said, his eyes terrible to

look into. He took a slow breath and turned
away, weary of the whole thing. "She died,"
he said again, almost to himself, as he went
back toward the truck.

"Mr. Fenton..." she called hesitantly,
aware that she'd hit a nerve and felt vaguely
ashamed of herself.

He turned and glared at her over the hood
of the truck. "I'll phone the manager of the
hotel in the morning and have him tell you
where to meet me for the next stop on the tour.
You can drive yourself from now on, Ms. Ma-
cho."

He got into the truck, slammed the door, and
took off in a cloud of dust.

She stared after him with conflicting emotions. It was important to stand on her own two
feet, not to be babied or pitied. She'd gone
overboard here, though, and she was sorry. He
was grieving for his lost love. He must have
cared very much. She wondered how the mys-
terious Anita had died, and why Mr. Fenton
looked so tormented when he spoke of her.

She went into the hotel with slow steps, feeling every step she took, hating her weakness
and her inability to do anything to correct it.

She reached the desk and smiled forcibly as she asked for her key.

The clerk, a personable young woman, handed it to her with an indifferent smile and turned away, pointedly disinterested in the breathless, bedraggled guest before her.

Candy laughed to herself. It was such a contrast from Guy Fenton's quiet concern. She hated having been so hateful to him, when he was only being compassionate. It was just that, over the years, she'd had so much pity and lurid curiosity, and so little love.

When she got to her room, she locked the door and fell onto the bed in a collapsed heap, without even taking her shoes off. A minute later, she was sound asleep.

The shots woke her. She sat up in bed, her heart hammering at her throat. She had a hand over her chest and she was shaking. More shots, more...

She was out in the open. There were no trees. There was nothing to hide behind. She felt a blow in her chest and touched it with her hand. It came away red, wet with fresh blood. The pain came behind it, wrenching pain. She couldn't breathe...

She threw herself down onto the ground and held her hands over her head. She saw blood. She saw blood everywhere! People were screaming. Children were screaming. A man in a clown suit went down with a horrible piercing scream. Beside her, she saw her father double over and fall, his eyes closed, closed, closed forever...

She wasn't aware that she was sobbing out loud until the angry shrill alarm on the bedside table began to permeate her sleep-drugged senses. Her eyes opened. She was lying on the cold floor, on the carpet, doubled up like a frightened child. She sucked in wind, trying desperately to get enough air in her lungs to breathe. She dragged herself into a sitting position and felt for the clock until she found the switch that cut off the loud alarm. She was wet with sweat, shivering, terrified. All those years ago, she thought, and the nightmares continued. She shivered once more, convulsively, and dragged herself back onto the bed, to lie with open eyes and a throbbing chest.

The nightmare was an old companion, one she'd managed for a long time. There were, fortunately, not so many maniacs running loose that her injury was a common one. But it did appeal to a certain type of person, who wanted her to recount that horror, to relive it. She couldn't bear the least reference to her breathlessness, because of bad memories about the media, hounding her and the other survivors just after the tragedy that had taken so many innocent lives that bright, sunny spring day ten years ago.

She put her face in her hands and wished she could squeeze her head hard enough to force the memory out of it forever. Her mother had withdrawn into a cold, self-contained shell just after her husband's funeral. Forced to assume control of the family ranch or give it up, she became a businesswoman. She hated cattle, but she loved the money they earned for her. Candy was an afterthought, a reminder of her terrible loss. She'd loved her husband more than anything on the face of the earth. Somehow she blamed Candy for it. The distance between mother and daughter had become a gap as wide as an ocean, and there seemed no way to bridge it. Candy's job was a lifesaver, because it got her out of Montana, away from the mother who barely tolerated her.

Mostly she liked her job as a cattle industry publicist. Unlike her mother, she did love cattle, and everything connected with them. She'd have enjoyed living on the ranch, but Ida hated the very sight of her and made no attempt to conceal it. It was better for both of them that Candy never went home these days.

She pushed back her damp hair and tried to think about the next day's adventure. They were going to see a rancher named Cy Parks, from all accounts the most unfriendly rancher in Jacobsville, a man with no tact, no tolerance for strangers, and more money than he knew what to do with. She was used to difficult men, so this would be just another check on her clipboard. But she was genuinely sorry that she'd been so unfriendly to Guy Fenton, who was only concerned for her. She should tell him about her past and then perhaps they could go from there. He wasn't a bad man. He had a sense of humor and a good brain. She wondered why he wasn't using it. He didn't seem the sort to tie himself for life to managing a feedlot. Surely he could have struck out on his own, started his own business.

She laid her head back on the damp pillow

with a grimace. Only a few more hours to daylight. She had sleeping pills, but she never took them. She hated the very thought of any sort of addiction. She didn't smoke or drink, and she'd never been in love. That required too much trust.

A glance at the bedside clock assured her that she had four hours left to stare at the light patterns on the ceiling or try to sleep. She closed her eyes with a sigh.

Guy Fenton, true to his word, called the motel and left a message for Candy, giving her directions to the Parks ranch and assuring her that he'd be there when she arrived. She was dreading the meeting, after the way she'd acted. He probably thought the worst of her after yesterday. She hoped she could undo the damage.

She drove up to the sprawling wood ranch house. The surroundings were well-kept, the white fences were painted, the corrals looked neat and clean, there was a huge barn out back with a fenced pasture on either side of it, and the paved driveway had obviously been landscaped, because there were flowering plants and shrubs and trees everywhere. Either Mr. Parks had inherited this place or he loved flowers. She wondered which.

He came out onto the porch with Guy to meet her, unsmiling and intimidating. She saw at once that none of her former experiences with difficult men had prepared her to deal with this tiger.

"Cy Parks, Candace Marshall," Guy introduced them curtly. "Ms. Marshall is interviewing local ranchers for a publicity spread in a national magazine to promote new ideas in beef management."

"Great idea," Cy said, but the smile he gave her wasn't pleasant. "The animal rights activists will use the platform for protests and the antimeat lobby will demand equal space for a rebuttal."

Candy's eyebrows lifted at the frontal attack. "We're trying to promote new methods," she replied. "Not start a food war."

"It's already started, or don't you watch daytime television?" Cy drawled coldly.

She let out a slow breath. *"Welll,"* she drawled, "we could just lie down on the highway voluntarily and let the other side pave us over.''

The corner of his wide mouth jerked, but there was no friendly light in those cold green eyes, and his lean face was harder than the tanned leather it resembled. He was Guy's height, but even slimmer, built like a rodeo cowboy with a cruel-looking mouth and big feet. He kept his left hand in his pocket, but with his right, he gestured toward the nearest pasture.

''If you want to see my new bull, he's that way,'' Cy said shortly. He came down the steps with a slow, lazy stride and led the way to the fenced area. ''He's already won competitions.''

Candy stared through the fence at the enormous animal. He was breathtaking, for a bull, with his shiny red coat and eye-catching conformation.

''Nothing to say?'' Cy chided.

She shook her head. ''I'm lost for words,'' she replied simply. ''He's beautiful.''

Cy made a rough sound in his throat, but he didn't take her up on the controversial description.

"I thought you might want to mention your, shall we say unorthodox, pest control methods," Guy prompted.

Cy's black eyebrows jerked under the wide brim of his hat. "I don't like pesticides," he said flatly. "They mess up the groundwater table. I use insects."

"Insects?" Candy had heard of this method, and she began to quote a magazine article she'd read recently about the use of beneficial insects to control pest insects on agricultural land.

"That's exactly where I found out about it," he replied, impressed. "I thought it was worth a try, and couldn't be worse than the stuff we were already using. I was pretty surprised with the results. Now I'm going organic on fertilizer as well." He nodded toward the heifers in a far pasture, safely removed from his bull. "Shame to waste all that by-product of my growing purebred herd," he added tongue-in-cheek. "Especially considering what city folk spend to buy it in bags. I don't even have to waste plastic."

Candy laughed. Her voice was musical, light, and Guy found himself staring at her. He hadn't heard her laugh, but here was the town's most hostile citizen and he amused her.

Cy didn't smile, but his green eyes did. "You should smile more," he said.

She shrugged. "Everybody should."

He bent his head toward her. "I saw your mother a few weeks ago at a convention. She's turned to ice, hasn't she?"

Her face was shocked. "Well, yes, I suppose…"

"Can't blame her," he said heavily. He searched Candy's eyes. "But it wasn't your fault."

"Everybody says that," she said shortly, all too aware of Guy's intent scrutiny.

"You should listen," he said shortly.

She nodded. "Now about that bull," she said, changing the subject.

Once on his favorite theme, he was good for several minutes. For a taciturn man, he was eloquent on the subject of that bull and all his good breeding points. He expanded until Candy had all she needed and walked quietly beside him while he showed them around the rest of the compound.

She was ready to leave shortly before Guy.

She shook hands with Cy Parks, nodded cautiously toward Guy, got in her rental car, and drove back to her motel.

Guy wasn't in such a big hurry. He paused by the fender of his pickup truck and turned toward Cy. "What happened to her?"

"Ask her," he said with customary bluntness.

"I could get more by asking the car she's riding in."

Cy shrugged. "I don't guess it's any real secret. About nine or ten years ago, her dad took her to a fast-food joint for lunch. You know, Dad and his little girl, sharing a meal and talking to each other. As it happened, that particular day the manager had fired an employee for drinking on the job. The guy was using drugs, too, but the manager didn't know that. So, there's everybody in the fast-food joint, talking and waiting for orders, including Candy and her dad, when this guy they fired comes in with an AK-47 assault rifle and starts shooting."

Guy caught his breath audibly. "Was she hit?"

Cy nodded solemnly. "In the chest. Destroyed one of her lungs and she almost died. They removed the lung. Her dad wasn't so lucky. He took a round in the face. Died instantly. They say that her mother never stopped blaming her for it. It was her idea to go there for lunch, you see.''

''And the mother assumed that if she hadn't wanted to go, Candy's father would still be alive.''

''Exactly.'' He stared toward the small dust cloud Candy's car was making in the distance. ''She's real touchy on the subject, they say. The media hounded her and her mother right after the shooting. Even now, some enterprising reporter turns up her name and wants to do an update. Her mother sued one of them for trespassing on her ranch and won. She doesn't get bothered much. I imagine Candy does.'' He shook his head. ''I hear that she and her mother barely speak these days. Apparently she's decided that if Mama doesn't want her around, she'll cooperate.''

''What's her mother like?''

Cy pursed his lips. ''The sort you can't imagine ever getting married. Most men walk wide around her. She's a sausage grinder. No inhibitions about speaking her mind, and that mind is sharp as a knife blade. Nothing like Candy, there,'' he added thoughtfully. ''She's all bluff. Underneath, she's marshmallow.''

Guy scowled. ''How do you know that?''

''I recognize a fellow sufferer,'' he said, and took his left hand out of his pocket.

Guy's eyebrows jerked, just a little, when he saw it. It wasn't disfigured, but it had very obviously been badly burned. The skin was slick and tight over it.

''Didn't anyone tell you that my Wyoming ranch burned to the ground?'' he asked the younger man. ''I don't suppose they added that I was in it at the time, with my wife and son?''

Guy felt sick to his stomach. It was painfully obvious that the other two members of the Parks family hadn't survived.

Cy looked at his hand, his jaw taut and his face hard. He put it back in the pocket and looked at Guy with dead eyes. ''It took three neighbors to drag me back out of the house. They sat on me until the firemen got inside. It was already too late. I'd gotten home late because of bad weather. There was a thunderstorm while I was finishing up some urgent paperwork in the office on one side of the house. The fire started in the other, where they were both asleep. Later, they said a lightning strike caused the fire.'' He stared into space with terrible eyes. ''My boy was five years...'' He stopped, turned away, breathed until his voice was steady again. ''I left Wyoming. Couldn't bear the memories. I thought I'd start again, here. Money was no problem, I've always had that. But time doesn't heal. Damn it...!''

Guy felt the man's pain and understood it. ''I was flying my fiancée around the county one afternoon,'' he said evenly. ''I thought I'd impress her with a barrel roll...but I stalled out. The plane went down, into some trees, and hung there by a thread with the passenger side facedown to the ground. I came to my senses and saw Anita there, hanging onto the seat with her feet dangling.'' His eyes grew cold. ''It must have been a good forty feet to the ground. She was crying, pleading with me not to let her fall. I reached down to catch her, and she let go with one hand to grab mine. She lost her hold.'' His eyes closed. ''I wake up in the night, seeing her face, contorted with fear, hear her voice crying out to me.'' His eyes opened and he drew in a breath. "I know what hell is. I've lived in it for three years. You don't get over it."

Cy winced. "I'm sorry."

"So am I, for you. But it doesn't help, does it?" he asked on cold laughter. He removed his hat, ran a hand through his hair, and put it back on again. "Well, I'll go chase up the publicity lady and carry on."

"Sure."

He lifted a hand and got into the truck. There was really nothing more to be said. But commiseration did ease the sting of things. Just a little.

Chapter 3

Guy followed Candy back to the motel, and found her car parked in front of one of the rooms on the end of the complex. He parked his truck beside it, got out, and rapped on her door.

She opened the door, looking pale and worn. She wasn't breathing very well, either.

"We can go out to Matt Caldwell's place tomorrow," he said at once. "If you don't mind," he added carefully, trying not to let his concern for her health show too much. "I've got a few things I need to do at the feedlot this afternoon, but if you're determined to carry on...?''

"No, it can...wait." She searched his face. "He told you about me, didn't he?" she added without preamble.

There seemed little reason to hedge. "Yes," he replied, with no trace of expression on his face. He continued as if he hadn't paid much attention to the subject. "I'll phone you in the morning. I've got a client coming to look over his cattle, and he'll want details about our feeding program that I'll have to explain to him. He's a lot like J. D. Langley—he doesn't like feedlots but he's working for a corporation that does. We're expecting him when we open for business, but if he comes later, I may have to let you go to Matt's place alone. If that happens, I'll fax a map over to the motel office and you can pick it up before you leave. His ranch is almost a half hour out of town on some real back roads. Some of them don't even have road signs!"

She was surprised that he didn't mention her past. She relaxed a little. "That will be fine," she said.

He watched her struggle for breath, and she

began to cough rather violently. "Have you ever been tested for asthma?" he persisted.

She held a tissue to her mouth while she fought the weakness that was making it hard for her to talk at all. "No."

"Well, you should be," he said bluntly, eyes narrow with concern. "Everybody says asthma makes you wheeze, but it doesn't always. I dated a girl last year who had it real bad, but she didn't wheeze, she just coughed until it sounded like her lungs might come up."

She leaned heavily against the door facing. "Why aren't you still dating her?" she asked.

"I let another woman flirt with me when we went on our first date," he replied. "We didn't have a lot in common, but I felt ashamed. I'm not usually that inconsiderate."

"Did she find somebody else?"

He chuckled. "She married her boss, one of our local doctors. My loss, but I think he was sweet on her from the beginning. He gave me hell about letting her go home alone from the theater."

She searched his eyes quietly. "Why do you get drunk every weekend?" she asked.

He was shocked, and looked it. "Who told you?" he asked impatiently.

"Mr. Gately, while you were looking at the horses," she replied. "He said to stay away from you on weekends, and I asked why."

He rammed his hands in his pockets and looked unapproachable. "My fiancée died in a plane crash. I was flying the plane. I stalled out the engine showing off, and I managed to get it down into the trees without killing us. But the tree we landed in was forty feet off the ground. Her seat belt came loose and she fell out before I could catch her." His eyes darkened with the memory. "I drink so I won't have to see her face as she fell out the door, or hear her scream for me to help her."

She crumpled the tissue in her hand. "I'm so sorry," she said gently. "So very sorry."

"I wouldn't have told you if I hadn't known what happened to you," he replied. "Some people love to hear about violent deaths. Maybe it makes them feel alive. It just makes me feel like getting drunk."

"I can understand that. But she wouldn't have wanted you to mourn that way, would she?"

He hesitated. "No. I don't suppose she would."

"Or live your life alone, either," she persisted. She smiled. "My father was like that, always doing for other people, bringing us little presents, taking care of us. He was much more nurturing than my mother ever was. Of course, now she hates me. I killed him, you see," she added tightly. "I was the one who suggested that we go to that particular place for lunch."

"It could have happened anywhere," he said.

She shrugged. "Sure it could, but it happened there. These days, I spend as little time at home as I can manage. I suppose I'm tired of paying for my sins." She laughed hollowly. "I run. You run. And they're still dead, aren't they?"

Her voice broke on the last word. He couldn't understand why it affected him the way it did, but he couldn't stand there and watch her cry.

He eased her into the motel room and closed the door behind them. He drew her into his arms and held her hard, tight, close against the length of him while his lean hand stroked her soft hair. She'd left it loose today, and it fell to her shoulders like dark silk. It smelled of flowers.

"I don't need..." she began, in just a token protest.

He smoothed the hair back from her face. "You do," he corrected. "So do I. It's human to want comfort."

"Do I?" she asked miserably.

"Yes. And I do, too."

He wrapped her up again and just stood there holding her while she clung to him, more at peace than he'd been in years. He liked the way she felt in his arms, warm and soft and vulnerable.

She sighed after a minute and nestled closer.

"Didn't your mother ever hug you?" he asked.

"Not really. She wasn't affectionate, except with Dad, and that was rare. She still isn't a touching person."

"Neither am I, as a rule." His chest lifted and fell against her. "What a hard little shell you wear, Ms. Marshall," he murmured against her temple.

"I don't want pity."

"Neither do I," he said. "But I could get used to being comforted."

She smiled against his shirt. "So could I."

"Suppose we give up fighting and declare a truce?"

Her heart jumped. "Isn't that cowardice under fire?"

"Not between two old troopers like us."

She smoothed her hand over his soft shirt. "I suppose I could try not to be on the defensive so much if you'll try not to get drunk."

He was still. His eyes went past her head to the big oak tree beside the motel. Absently, he wondered how old it was. "I haven't tried going without alcohol in a long time," he confided. "Even if just on weekends. But I'd have to have an alternative."

Her fingers toyed with a pearl button midway down his chest. "I don't suppose you like fishing."

He lifted his head. "You're kidding, of course."

"Do you or don't you?" she asked, perplexed.

"I won the bass rodeo last year."

Her eyebrows went up and she chuckled. "Only because I wasn't competing with you," she said. "I love to fish for bass!"

A soul mate, he was thinking. He almost said it aloud. "I'll bet you didn't bring your tackle with you."

She grimaced. "I had to fly here. I couldn't carry everything I wanted to."

"I'll kit you out. I've got spinning reels and cane poles, everything from sinkers to hooks to floats. We'll spend Saturday at the lake."

"I'd love to!" She smiled up at him with her soft eyes, and he wondered why he'd ever thought she was cold.

"I'll try to get somebody to substitute for me so I can go with you to Matt's in the morning. About nine suit you? I'll arrange it with him, too."

"That will be fine. Is he like Cy Parks?" she asked, curious.

He shook his head. "Matt's easygoing most of the time, unless he's really mad and then people get out of his way. He likes women. As a rule," he added.

"There's an exception, I gather?"

"Only one." He smiled at her. "I'll see you

tomorrow. You might try some strong coffee,'' he suggested. "They say it helps an asthma attack—if that's what you're having. If you don't get better, call the doctors Coltrain or Dr. Morris. They're all great.''

"Okay. Thanks.''

He let her go with a sigh. "It's not a weakness to get help when you're sick,'' he mused. "I just thought I'd mention that.''

"I wasn't allowed to be sick at home,'' she told him. "Some lessons are hard to unlearn.''

He searched her wan face. "What a childhood you must have had,'' he said sadly.

"It was all right, until my dad died.''

"I wonder,'' he mused, unconvinced.

She coughed again, holding the handkerchief to her mouth.

He scowled. "That wheat straw dust gets to you, doesn't it?'' he asked with concern. "You need to stay out of enclosed places where it's bad. If you really do have asthma, it's dangerous.''

"I have one lung,'' she said huskily. "It's sensitive to dust, I guess.''

He wasn't buying it. "I'll call you tonight,

just to make sure you're okay. If it doesn't get better, call the doctor or get to the hospital.''

"I will. You don't need to worry.''

"Somebody does,'' he said curtly. "If you're not better in the morning, we might put Matt off until you are. He lives in town, but his ranch is about twenty-five minutes out of town. If you had a life-threatening attack out there, I'd never get you to town in time in the truck.''

"Mr. Caldwell has an airplane,'' she pointed out.

"He has two—a Learjet and a little Cessna Commuter,'' he replied, "but he's only going to be at the ranch long enough to introduce us to his ranch manager. He's flying himself to Fort Worth in the Learjet for a conference.''

"I'll be fine by the morning,'' she said doggedly. "I know I will.'' She ruined the stoic image with another choking cough.

"Go drink some coffee, just to humor me, will you?''

She sighed. "Okay.''

"Good girl.'' He bent abruptly and put his mouth gently against hers.

She jumped and a shocked breath pulsed out of her.

He searched her eyes curiously. "You aren't afraid of me, are you?" he asked gently.

"I don't...think so."

Her attitude was surprising. She seemed confident and self-assured, until he came intimately close. She didn't seem to know a lot about men.

"Don't people kiss you, either?" he asked.

"Not a lot."

"Pity," he said, glancing down at her mouth. "You've sure got the mouth for kissing—soft and warm and very sweet."

She put her hand to it, unconsciously. "I don't like sports," she said absently.

"What's that got to do with kissing?"

"Most of the men I meet are married, but the ones who aren't want to take me to football or baseball games. I like fishing."

"I like sports," he mused. "But mostly rodeo and fishing."

"I like rodeo, too."

"See? Something we have in common, already," he said with a smile. He bent and brushed his mouth against hers again, feeling the same faintly electric sensation as before. He grinned as his lips teased hers. "I could get addicted to this."

She put her hands on his chest. "I can't... breathe very well," she whispered. "I'm sorry."

He lifted his head and stared down at her. "Is that why you don't get involved? You can't get your breath and when you mention it, men think you're giving them the brush-off?"

"How did you know?" she asked, surprised.

"It's the obvious answer to your lack of marriageable suitors," he said simply. "It certainly isn't due to a lack of looks. Why didn't you tell them you only had one lung?"

She grimaced. "It wouldn't have mattered very much. They wanted a lot more than a few kisses."

"And you didn't."

She shook her head. "I've been dead inside since my father died. The psychologist they sent me to afterward said it was guilt because he died and I didn't. Maybe it's still that way." She looked up at him. "But regardless of the guilt, I just don't feel that way with most men. Well, I haven't...before.''

She was flushing and he knew why. He grinned, feeling ten feet tall. ''It's like little electric shocks, isn't it?'' he mused.

She smiled shyly. ''Sort of.''

He pursed his lips. ''Care to try for a major lightning strike?''

She laughed. ''Not today.''

''Okay.'' He pushed back a stray strand of her hair, admiring its softness. ''I'll see you in the morning, then.''

''I'll look forward to it.''

He sobered. ''So will I.'' There was an odd little glitter in his eyes. It grew as he looked at her. It was almost as if he had to jerk his eyes away from hers and force himself to move away. In fact, that's exactly how it was. He liked women, and from time to time he was attracted to them. It hadn't been like this. He wanted this woman in ways he'd never wanted any other.

He hesitated as he reached the truck. ''I meant it about the doctor,'' he said with genuine concern. ''If that cough doesn't stop, see someone.''

"All right." She smiled, waved, and closed the door.

He drove away, but not without misgivings. He didn't like the way she looked when that cough racked her. She was fragile, but she didn't realize it or just plain ignored it. She needed someone to take care of her. He smiled at the random thought. That was certainly an outdated notion. Women didn't like being taken care of. They wanted to be independent and strong. But he wondered if they didn't secretly like the idea of being nurtured by someone—not controlled, dominated, or smothered, but just...nurtured.

He thought of her as an orchid that needed just the right amount of attention—a growth mixture of bark, a little careful watering now and then—to make it grow. Orchids needed lots of humidity and cool nights. He smiled at the thought of Candy letting him put her in a pot and pour water over her. But it was the sort of thing he wanted, to take care of her and never let her be hurt again. He scowled, because the things he was thinking were very much against his nature. He was a loner. He'd never thought much about nurturing anything, much less a woman. He couldn't think of Candy any other way, and he'd known her only a matter of days.

It was too soon to be thinking of anything permanent, he assured himself. All the same, it wouldn't hurt to keep an eye on her. He had a feeling that she was going to form a very large part of his future happiness.

Back in the motel, Candy had finally gotten the best of the raging cough by stifling it with a large pot of strong black coffee. She hadn't expected results, despite Guy's assurances about coffee being good for asthma, but apparently he was right. She frowned. If she did have asthma, it was going to complicate her life. Working around ranches and wheat straw dust and grain dust was going to constitute a major challenge, even if there was a reliable treatment for it.

She sipped her coffee and thought about Guy's concern, about the way he took care of her. She was a modern woman, of course she was. But it felt nice, having somebody care what happened to her. Her mother didn't. Nobody had cared what happened to her since her

father died. She couldn't help being touched
by Guy's concern—and wasn't that an about-
face from his first attempts at it, she asked herself wryly.

Later, just before she went to bed, the phone
rang. It was Guy, just checking on her. She
told him that she was all right and he told her
that he'd found someone to handle the visiting
cattleman for him. He'd see her in the morning.

He hung up and she held on to the receiver
for a long time before she put it down. It
wasn't bad, having somebody care about her.
It wasn't bad at all.

The next morning dawned bright and beautiful. Candy dressed in a neat beige pantsuit
and suede boots for the trip, leaving her hair
loose. She felt younger and happier than she
had in years. She had a whole new outlook on
life because of Guy.

She reviewed her few facts on the Caldwell
ranch. It was only one of a dozen pies Matt
had his finger in. He was an entrepreneur in
the true sense of the word, an empire-builder.
If he'd been born a hundred years ago, he'd

have been a man like Richard King, who founded the famous King Ranch in southeastern Texas. Matt was an easygoing, pleasant man to most people. She'd heard that he was hell in boots to his enemies. There were always rumors about such a powerful man, and one of them was that he had it in for a female friend of his cousin's and had caused her to lose her job. It was a glaring black mark against a man who was generally known for fair play, and people talked about it. She was a very young woman, at that, not at all the sort of female the handsome tycoon was frequently seen with.

Matt's taste ran to models and Hollywood stars. He had no use for high-powered career women in his private life, although he employed several in executive positions in his various companies. Perhaps that was why the young woman had run afoul of his temper, Candy speculated. She was rumored to be very intelligent and sharp at business.

A rap on the motel door startled her. She went to answer it and found a smiling Guy on the doorstep.

"Ready to go?"

"Oh, yes!" she said brightly. The day had taken a definite turn for the better.

Matt's sprawling ranch lay about twenty-five minutes out of town, and it was truly out in the boondocks.

Guy took a road that wasn't identified in any way and flashed a grin at Candy. "I'm afraid even a good map wouldn't have helped much. Matt says he likes being someplace where he's hard to find, but it's hell on people who have to go out here on business."

"He must not like people," she commented.

"He does, in fact, but not when he's in a black mood. That's when he comes out here. He works right alongside his cowhands and the newer ones sometimes don't even realize he's the boss until they see him in a suit and boarding the Learjet. He's just one of the boys."

"How rich is he?" she asked.

He chuckled. "Nobody knows. He owns this ranch and a real estate franchise, two planes, he has property in Australia and Mexico, he's on the board of directors of four companies and on the board of trustees of two universities. In his spare time, he buys and sells cattle.'' He shook his head. ''I've never known a man with so much energy.''

''Does he do it to get his mind off something?'' she wondered aloud.

''Nobody's ever had the nerve to ask. Matt's very pleasant, but he isn't the sort of man you question.''

She bumped along beside him in the truck and something nagged at the back of her mind.

''You said you were flying the plane. Did you own it?'' she asked carefully.

He drew in a slow breath. He didn't want to talk about it, but then, she was entitled to know something about him. He glanced at her. ''I did. I have an air cargo company.''

Her eyes widened. ''And you're working for wages at a feedlot?''

''They don't know I own the company,'' he told her. ''I wanted someplace to... I don't know, hide out maybe.'' He shrugged broad shoulders. ''I couldn't cope with the memories there, and I didn't want enough spare time to think. I got the most demanding job I could find. I've been here three years and I like it. My manager is doing great things with the air cargo company. I'm considering making him a full partner.''

"Is it a profitable company?''

"I'm not in Matt Caldwell's league,'' he said. "But I suppose I'm pretty close.'' He glanced at her and smiled. "I could afford to live high if I liked. I don't. I was too fond of the fast lane. It's what cost me Anita.'' His face tautened as he stared ahead at the long, winding road. "I'd been on the road all of the day before, and I hadn't slept that night because someone had a party and I was enjoying myself. Anita wanted to go up for a few minutes, so I took her. If I'd had a good night's sleep, I wouldn't have done such a sketchy walk-around and I'd have noticed the problem in the engine before it caused a tragedy. That was when I looked at my life and decided that I was wasting it. I came down here to decide what to do.'' He shook his head. "It's been three years and I still haven't decided that.''

"What do you want to do?'' she asked.

His eyes held a faraway look. "I want to settle down and have a family.'' He saw the expression on her face and chuckled. "I can see that you hadn't considered that answer as a possibility."

"You don't seem the sort of man to want to settle," she said evasively. She twisted her purse in her lap.

"I wasn't, until recently. I'm not that old, but I'm beginning to see down the road further than I used to. I don't want to grow old and die alone."

"Most people don't."

He grinned. "Including you?"

She hesitated. "I'd never really thought about marrying and having a family," she said seriously.

"Because you only have one lung? That shouldn't worry you."

"It might worry a prospective husband," she pointed out. "Most men want a whole woman."

"You're whole, in every way that matters," he said firmly. "With or without two lungs."

She smiled. "Thanks. That was nice. But marriage is a big step."

"Not really. Not if two people have a lot in common and if they're good friends. I've seen some very happy marriages since I moved to

Jacobsville. Marriage is what you make of it,"
he said pensively.

"So they say."

The road dead-ended at a long, winding
gravel driveway with a huge black mailbox at
the fork which read Caldwell Double C Ranch.

"We're almost there," Guy told her, pulling
into the ranch road. "Matt runs some of the
prettiest Santa Gertrudis cattle in the state. It's
a purebred herd, which means they aren't
slaughter cattle. He sells seed bulls and heifers,
mostly, and he does a roaring business."

"I like Santa Gerts," she remarked.

"So did my father," he told her. "He
worked on the King Ranch. I grew up with
cattle and always loved them. I just loved airplanes more. Now I'm caught between the two.
That tickles my parents."

"They're still alive?"

He chuckled. "Very. He still works on a
ranch, and she's gone into real estate! I go to
visit them every few months." He glanced at
her. "As I mentioned before, I have a brother
in California and a sister in Washington State.
She has a little boy about four. Her husband's
a lawyer."

"Quite a family," she mused.

"You'd like my family," he told her. "They're just plain folks, nothing put on or fancy, and they love company."

"My mother screams about uninvited guests," she recalled. "She's not really fond of people unless they come to buy cattle. She's pretty mercenary."

"You aren't."

She laughed. "Thanks for noticing. No, I'll never make a businesswoman. If I had a lot of money, I'd probably give it all away. I'm a sucker for a lost cause."

"That makes two of us. And here we are."

He indicated a sprawling white two-story ranch house with a porch that ran two-thirds of the way around it. There was a porch swing and plenty of chairs and gliders to sit in. The pasture fences near the house were all white, and behind them red-coated cattle grazed on green grass.

"Improved pasture," she murmured, taking notes. "You can always tell by the lush grass."

"Matt's a stickler for improvements. There

he is.'' He nodded toward the front steps,
where a tall, darkly handsome man in a suit
and a white Stetson was coming down to greet
them.

Chapter 4

Matt Caldwell was attractive, and he had a live wire personality to go with his lean good looks. He helped Candy from the truck with a charm that immediately captivated her.

"Glad you got here before I had to leave," Matt said, greeting Guy as he came around the truck. "I'm going to have Paddy show you the place. I wish I could, but I'm already late for a meeting in Houston." He glanced at his watch. "I never have a minute to spare these days. I think I need to slow down."

"It wouldn't hurt," Guy chuckled. "Candy Marshall, this is Matt Caldwell."

"Glad to meet you," Candy said with a smile and an extended hand.

Matt shook it warmly. "Publicists are getting neater by the day," he mused. "The last one we had here was twenty-five, unshaven, and didn't know a Santa Gert from a Holstein."

"I shaved my beard off just this morning," she said pertly.

Matt chuckled. "Glad to know that you have good personal hygiene," he drawled. "Paddy will show you anything you want to see. If you need to talk to me, I should be back by tomorrow morning. If that's not soon enough, you can fax me the questions, I'll answer them and fax them back to you." He handed her a business card with Mather Caldwell Enterprises, Inc. in raised black lettering.

"Impressive," she told him.

He chuckled. "Not very." He glanced at Guy with a calculating gleam in his eyes. "If you wanted to give her a bird's-eye view of the ranch, the Cessna Commuter 150's gassed up and ready to fly."

Guy's face went hard just thinking about the small, two-seater plane. It was the type he'd crashed three years ago taking Anita for a ride. "I don't fly anymore."

Matt exchanged a complicated glance with him. "Pity."

"She wants to see cattle on the hoof, anyway."

"I bought a new Santa Gertrudis bull from the King Ranch. Paddy will show him to you. He's a looker." Matt shook hands with them both. "Got to run," he said. "Paddy should be out here any minute. He was with me when you drove up, but he got held up in the office. Have a seat on the porch and wait for him."

"Nice porch," Candy remarked.

He grinned. "I bought the place for the porch. I like to sit out there on warm summer evenings and listen to Rachmaninoff."

He piled into his Mercedes and gunned the engine as he drove out to the small hangar and airstrip that were barely visible in the distance.

"Does he do that often? Offer you his airplane, I mean?" Candy asked when they were comfortably seated in the porch swing.

"Every time he sees me," he said with resignation. "I suppose I'm getting used to it. Which doesn't mean I like it," he added.

She didn't quite know how to answer that. It was a good thing that Paddy Kilgraw chose that moment to come out onto the porch. He was a wizened little man with skin like leather and twinkling blue eyes. He took off his hat, revealing pale red hair on either side of a huge bald spot, and shook hands warmly with them both. He led them out to the barn and Candy got down to business.

Matt's operation was enormous, but it still had the personal touch. He knew each of his bulls by name, and at least two of them were tame. Candy enjoyed the way they nuzzled her hand when she petted them. To her mother, cattle were for slaughter, nothing else. Candy much preferred a ranch that concentrated on keeping them alive, where the owner liked his animals and took proper care of them. Even cantankerous Cy Parks, who did run beef cattle, was concerned for their welfare and never treated them as if they were nothing more than an investment.

But the barn, while neat and clean for such a structure, was filled with wheat straw, and it was strictly an enclosed space. They'd barely entered it when Candy started coughing. She bent over double and couldn't stop.

Guy asked Paddy for a cup of coffee, which the little man went running to get. Meanwhile, Guy lifted Candy and carried her out of the barn, to where the air was less polluted by wheat straw dust. But once outside, seated on the running board of the truck, she was still coughing. Tears were running down her face, which was red as fire.

Paddy appeared with a cup of coffee. "It's cold, will that do?" he asked quickly.

"Cold is fine. It's the caffeine we want." Guy held it to her lips, but she was coughing so hard that she couldn't even drink in between spasms. His face contorted with fear. He looked up at Paddy from his kneeling position beside Candy. "I think it's a bad asthma attack," he said abruptly.

"Has she got an inhaler on her?" Paddy asked.

Guy shook his head worriedly. "She hasn't been diagnosed by a doctor yet. Damn!"

She bent over again, and this time she was definitely wheezing as she coughed. It was getting worse by the second and she looked as if she was struggling to get a single breath of air.

"It's twenty-five minutes to Jacobsville!" Guy said harshly. "I'll never get her there in time!"

"Take the Commuter," Paddy said. "I've got the keys in my pocket. Boss said you might like to fly her while you were here."

Guy's eyes were haunted. "Paddy, I can't!" he bit off, horror in his expression at the memory of his last flight.

Paddy put a firm hand on his shoulder. "Her life depends on it," he reminded the younger man solemnly. "Yes, you can! Here. Go!"

Guy took another look at Candy and groaned. He took the keys from Paddy, put Candy in the truck, swung in beside her, and gunned the engine out to the airstrip, with Paddy hanging on in the truck bed.

He pulled the truck to a stop at the hangar. Leaving Candy in the cab of the truck, Guy and Paddy got the little Cessna pulled out onto the apron. Then Guy carried Candy and strapped her into the passenger side. She was barely conscious, her breath rasping as she tried desperately to breathe.

"You'll make it," Paddy said firmly. "I'll phone ahead and have an ambulance and EMTs waiting at the airport in Jacobsville with the necessary equipment. Get going!"

"Thanks, Paddy," Guy called as he ran to get inside the plane.

It had been a long time since he'd flown, but it was like riding a bicycle, it came right back to him. He went over the controls and gauges and switches after he'd fired up the engine. He taxied the little plane out onto the runway and said a silent prayer.

"It's going to be all right, honey," he told Candy in a harsh tone. "Try to hang on. I'll have you to the hospital in no time in this!"

She couldn't manage a reply. She felt as if she were drowning, unable to get even a breath of air. She gripped the edge of the seat, crying silently, terrified, as Guy sent the little aircraft zipping down the runway and suddenly into the air.

He circled and turned the plane toward Jacobsville, thanking God for his skill as a pilot that had made this trip even possible. He could see that Candy was slowly turning blue and losing consciousness.

"Just a little longer, sweetheart," he pleaded above the noise of the engine. "Just a little longer! Please hold on!"

He kept talking to her, soothing her, encouraging her all the way to the Jacobsville airport. He was so preoccupied with her welfare that his horror of flying took a back seat to his concern for Candy. He called the tower and was immediately given clearance to land, which he did, faultlessly. An ambulance pulled onto the tarmac, lights flashing, and came to a halt as he taxied onto the apron and cut the engine.

Seconds later, they had Candy out of the plane and on oxygen. They loaded her into the ambulance, with one EMT and a worried Guy in the back with her. They roared away to the hospital, with Guy holding her hand and praying silently that he wasn't going to lose her, when he'd only just found her.

Her color was better and she was breathing less strenuously when the ambulance pulled up sharply at the emergency entrance. The physician on duty came running out behind the nurses and supervised Candy's entrance.

Guy was gently put to one side while Candy

was wheeled right into the emergency room, into a cubicle.

"You can sit here in the waiting area," a nurse told him with a gentle smile. "Don't worry. She's going to be fine."

Easy to say, he thought worriedly. He jammed his hands into the pockets of his jeans and paced, oblivious to the other people also waiting and worrying nearby. He couldn't remember the last time he'd been so upset.

He glanced toward the swinging doors through which Candy had been taken and sighed. She'd looked a little better after the oxygen mask was put into place, but he knew it was going to take more than that to get her back on her feet. He was almost certain that they'd keep her overnight. He hoped they would. She was stubborn and unlikely to follow instructions.

Just when he was contemplating storming the doors, the physician came and motioned him inside.

He pulled him into an empty cubicle and closed the curtain. "Is she your fiancée?" he asked Guy.

He shook his head. "She's a visiting pub-

licist for the cattlemen's association. I was
deputized by our local association to escort her
around the area ranches.''

"Damn!" the doctor muttered.

"Why? What's wrong?"

He glowered. "She's got the worst case of
asthma I've come across in years, and she
won't believe it. I've got her on a nebulizer
now, but she's going to need a primary care
physician to evaluate and treat her, or this isn't
going to be an isolated incident. She needs to
see someone right away. But I can't convince
her."

Guy smiled wryly. "Leave it to me," he
murmured. "I think I'm beginning to know
how to handle her. Is this a long-standing condition, do you think?"

"Yes, I do. The coughing threw her off.
Most people don't associate it with asthma, but
while it's not as common as wheezing, it is
certainly a symptom. I've prescribed a rescue
inhaler for her to carry, and told her that she
needs to be on a preventative. Her own doctor
can prescribe that."

"She lives in Denver," Guy said. "I'm not
sure she goes to a doctor regularly."

"She'd better," the young man said flatly. "She almost got here too late. Another few minutes and it would have been touch and go."

"I figured that," Guy said quietly.

"She owes you her life," he continued.

"She owes me nothing, but I'm going to make sure that she takes care of herself from now on."

"I'm glad to hear it."

"May I see her?"

He smiled and nodded. "Sure. She won't be able to talk. She's very busy."

"Good. She can listen better. I've got a lot to tell her."

The doctor only chuckled. He led the way into a larger cubicle where a worn-looking Candy was inhaling something in a mask that covered part of her face. She glanced at him and looked irritated.

"Asthma," Guy said, plopping down onto a stool nearby. "I told you, didn't I?"

She couldn't speak, but her eyes did. They were eloquent.

"He says you need to see a doctor and get the asthma treated."

She tugged at the mask. "I won't!"

"You will," he replied, putting it firmly back in place. "Committing suicide is not sensible."

She struck the side of the examination couch with her hand.

"I know, you don't want any more complications," he said for her. "But this could have cost you dearly. You have to take precautions, so that it doesn't happen again."

Her eyes seemed to brighten. She shifted and shook her head.

"Hay and wheat and ranches sort of go together," Guy said. "If you're going to spend any time around them, you have to have proper care. I'm going to make sure you get it."

She gave him a look that said him and what army?

He chuckled. "We'll go into that later. Getting easier to breathe?"

She hesitated, and then nodded. She searched his eyes and made a flying motion with her hand. She tugged the mask aside for a second. "I'm sorry...you had to do that. Are you...all right?"

He put the mask back in place again,

touched by her concern for him at such a traumatic time for herself. "Yes, I'm all right," he said. "I didn't have time to think about myself and my fears. I was too busy trying to save you. It wasn't as bad as I thought it would be. Of course," he added with a faint smile, "I was pretty preoccupied at the time."

"Thank you," she said in a ghostly, hoarse tone.

"Don't talk. Breathe."

She sighed. "Okay."

The nebulizer took a long time to empty. By the time she'd breathed in the last of the bronchodilator, she was exhausted. But she could get her breath again.

The doctor came back in and reiterated what he'd said about seeing a physician for treatment of her asthma.

He gave her a sample inhaler and a prescription for another, plus another prescription. "This one—" he tapped it "—is for what we call a spacer. It's a more efficient way of delivering the medicine than a pocket inhaler. You're to follow the directions. And as soon as possible, you get treatment. I don't want to

see you back in here again in that condition,"
he added with a smile to soften the words.

"Thank you," she said.

He shrugged. "That's what we're here for."
He frowned. "You never knew you had
asthma. I find that incredible. Don't you have
a family physician?"

"I only go to the clinic when I'm sick," she
said shortly. "I don't have a regular doctor."

"Find one," the physician recommended
bluntly. "You're a tragedy waiting to happen."

He shook hands with Guy and left them in
the cubicle.

Guy helped her to her feet and escorted her
to the clerk, where she gave her credit card and
address to the woman in charge.

"No insurance, either?" he asked.

She shrugged. "It never seemed necessary."

"You need taking in hand."

She shook her head. "Not tonight. I'm too
tired to fight. I want to go back to the motel."

He didn't like that idea at all. He worried
about her, being alone at night. "You
shouldn't be by yourself," he said uneasily. "I
could get a nurse to come and stay with you."

"No!" she said vehemently. "I can take care of myself!"

"Don't get upset," he said firmly. "It won't help matters. It could even bring on another attack."

She drew in a shaky breath. "I'm sorry. It scared me."

"That makes two of us," he confided. "I've never moved so fast in my life." He caught her hand in his and held it tight. "Don't do that again," he added in a strained tone.

She turned to him as they made it into the sunlight. "How do we get to the motel?" she asked worriedly. "And what about your truck?"

"Paddy will take good care of the truck. We have a taxi service here. We can use it," he added with a smile. "Come on. I need to make arrangements to return the plane and then I'll see that you get where you want to go. Eventually," he added under his breath.

Candy expected the cab to take them to the motel, but the address Guy gave the driver wasn't the motel after all. It was a doctor's office.

"Now see here…!" she began.

Her protests didn't cut any ice. He paid the driver and frog-marched her into Drew Morris's waiting room. The receptionist who'd replaced Drew's wife, Kitty, smiled at them.

Guy explained the problem, and the receptionist had them take a seat. But only a couple of minutes later, they were hustled into a cubicle.

Drew Morris came right in. He ignored Candy's protests and examined her with his stethoscope. Seconds later, he wrapped the stethoscope around his neck, sat back on the couch, and folded his arms.

"I'm not your physician, but I'll do until you get one. I'm going to give you a prescription for a preventative medicine. You use it along with the inhaler the emergency room doctor gave you."

"How did you know about that?" Candy asked, aghast.

"Guy called me before he called the cab," Drew said nonchalantly. "You use both medicines. If the medicines stop working, for any reason, don't increase the dosage—call me or get to the emergency room. You had a life-threatening episode today. Let it be a warning. You can control asthma, you can't cure it. You have to prevent these attacks.''

She gave in gracefully. "Okay," she said. "I'll do what I'm told."

"Have you had problems like this before?"

She nodded. "Quite a bit. I thought it was just a mild allergy. Nobody in my family has any sort of lung problem."

"It doesn't have to be inherited. Some people just get it—more today than ever before, especially children. It's becoming a major problem, and I'm convinced that pollution has something to do with it."

"What about my job?" she asked miserably. "I love what I do."

"What do you do?" Drew asked.

"I go around to ranches and interview people on their production methods. There's always a grain elevator, a storage silo, a barnful of hay or wheat straw—they're unavoidable."

"Then wear a mask and use your inhalants before you go near those pollutants," Drew said. "No reason you can't keep doing your job. People with asthma have won Olympic medals. It won't get you down unless you let it.''

She smiled at him. "You're very encouraging."

"I have to be. My wife, Kitty, is asthmatic."

"How is Kitty?" Guy asked.

He chuckled. "Pregnant," he murmured, and his high cheekbones colored. "We couldn't be happier."

"Congratulations," Guy said. "And thanks for having a look at Candy."

"My pleasure," Drew replied, and not without a noticeable speculation as his gaze went from one of them to the other.

"He seems to know you very well," Candy mentioned when the cab was carrying them back to her motel.

"He does. I used to date his wife, before she was his wife," he said. "I told you about her. She coughed instead of wheezed."

"Oh, yes, I remember." She didn't like the memory. Guy had apparently done a lot of dating locally, despite his grief at losing his fiancée.

"Kitty was sweet and gentle, and I liked her a lot," he continued. "But she loved Drew.

I'm glad they made it. He was grieving for his late wife. People around here never thought he'd marry again. I guess Kitty came up on his blind side.''

"He's nice."

"Yes, but like all our doctors around here, he's got a temper.'' He glanced at her pocketbook and leaned forward and told the cabdriver to stop at the nearby pharmacy. "You need to get those filled. We'll wait for them and call a cab when they're filled.''

"I could do it tomorrow," Candy began.

"No," he said, leaning over the seat to talk to the cabdriver.

They stopped and got the prescriptions filled and then went on to the motel. Guy left Candy in her room reluctantly and made sure that she had a bucket of ice and some soft drinks before he left, so that she wouldn't have to go out to get them.

"Try to get some rest," he said.

"But we didn't get to see all of Matt's ranch," she protested, frowning. "How will I ever write the story?"

"Matt said he could fax you the answers to any questions you didn't get answered at the ranch," he replied. "I'll explain the situation

to him and you can work up some questions.
I'll make sure he gets them.''

"That's really nice of you," she said.

He smiled down at her, feeling protective
and possessive all at once. "This could be
habit-forming, too, you know."

"What could?"

"Taking care of you," he said softly. He
bent and brushed his mouth tenderly against
hers. "Lie down and rest for a while. I'll come
back and get you and take you out to eat, if
you're up to it."

She grimaced. "I want to," she said. "But
I'm so tired, Guy."

She did look tired. Her face was drawn and
there were new lines around her mouth and
eyes. He traced one of them lightly.

"Suppose I bring something over to you?"
he asked. "What would you like?"

"Pork lo mein," she said at once.

He grinned. "My favorite. I'll see you about
six."

"Okay."

He finished his chores at the feedlot, having
had Paddy drive his truck back to town. He
drove Paddy home and then went to get supper

for Candy. He took the food to the motel. They ate silently and then rented an action film on the pay per view channel and piled up together on one of the double beds to watch it.

In no time at all, Candy was curled up against him sound asleep. He held her that way, marveling at the wonder of their closeness, at her vulnerability and his own renewed strength. He hadn't thought seriously about getting involved with anyone since he'd lost Anita, but Candy had slipped so naturally into his life that he accepted her presence with no misgivings at all.

He looked down at her with soft, possessive eyes. He didn't want to go back to the feedlot. He wanted to stay here with her, all night long. But if he did that, he'd compromise her. He couldn't risk that. She might not want commitment so soon. He wondered about the sanity of getting mixed up with a woman who lived several states away, but he couldn't talk himself out of it.

He knew at that moment that she had a hold on him that no distance, no circumstance, could break. And he was afraid.

Chapter 5

Guy bent and kissed Candy's closed eyes, brushing his lips against them until they fluttered and lifted.

She looked up at him drowsily, but with absolute trust. Involuntarily, her arms snaked up around his neck and she pulled him down to kiss him slowly, tenderly, on his hard mouth.

He groaned, and she felt him move, so that his body shifted next to hers. The kiss grew in pressure and insistence until one long leg slid right between both of hers and his mouth demanded.

She pushed at his chest, frightened by the sudden lack of breathable air.

His head lifted. He breathed roughly, but he understood without speaking why she'd drawn back. "Sorry," he whispered. His mouth moved to her chin, her neck, and into the opening her blouse left. His lean fingers unfastened buttons, so that his mouth could move down past her collarbone and onto even softer flesh.

Her hands picked at his shirt, hesitated, as new sensations lanced through her. She loved the feel of his mouth. She didn't protest as he eased the lacy strap off her shoulder, and his mouth trespassed on flesh that had never known a man's touch before.

She yielded immediately, arching up to meet his lips, pushing the fabric aside to make way for it. She felt his mouth over her hard nipple and its sudden moist pressure made her moan with pleasure.

He lifted his head and looked where his mouth had touched. He traced the firm rise sensually and bent to kiss it once more, lovingly, before he righted the lacy strap and buttoned the blouse again.

Her eyes asked a question.

He smiled and bent to kiss her tenderly.
"We have all the time in the world for that,"
he whispered. "Right now, you're a little
wounded bird and I have to take care of you."

Tears stung her eyes. She'd never had ten-
derness. It was new and overpowering.

He kissed the tears away. "Don't cry," he
murmured. "You're going to be fine now. Just
fine. Nothing bad is ever going to happen to
you as long as I'm around."

She clung to him hard, burying her face in
his throat as the tears fell even more hotly.

"Oh, Candy," he murmured huskily. He
held her close, rocked her in his arms, until
she had her self-control back. Then he got up
from the bed and pulled her up beside him, to
hold her carefully close.

"Sorry," she murmured on a sob. "I guess
I'm tired."

"So am I." He brushed his mouth against
her pert nose. "I'm going back to the feedlot.
Can I get you anything before I go?"

She shook her head. She smiled hesitantly.
"How about that fishing trip tomorrow?"

He smiled. "I'm game if you are."

"I'll use my medicines," she said without enthusiasm.

"You sure will, or we won't go," he assured her.

She wrinkled her nose at him. "Spoilsport."

"I hate emergency rooms," he said simply. "We have to keep you out of them."

"I'll try."

"Good."

"Thank you for saving my life," she said solemnly. "I know it must have brought back some terrible memories for you, having to fly again."

He wouldn't admit that. He wasn't going to think about it. He only smiled at her, in a vague, pleasant way. "Get some sleep. I'll see you bright and early tomorrow. If you feel like going, we'll go. If not, we'll find some other way to pass the time. Okay?"

She smiled wearily. "Okay."

He left her and went back to the bunkhouse at the feedlot, but he didn't sleep. Over and over again he saw Anita's face. He groaned as he finally just got up and forgot trying to make the memories go away. It was useless.

The next morning, Guy and Candy went fishing on the river, with cane poles and a bait bucket. It was, she muttered, absolutely primitive to try to catch a fish in such a manner.

He only grinned. He'd made a small fire and he had a frying pan heating. He was going to treat her to fresh fish for lunch.

It was a good idea, except that they sat on the riverbank for three hours and at the end of it they had yellow fly bites and mosquito bites, and not one fish between them.

"It must have been this prehistoric fishing gear," Candy remarked with a glowering look. "The fish probably laughed so hard that they sank to the bottom!"

"It isn't prehistoric," he said. "It gives fish a sporting chance."

She waved her hand at the river. "Some sporting chance! And whoever uses worms to catch a self-respecting bass?"

"You just wait until the next bass rodeo, pilgrim," he said with a mocking smile. "And we'll see who can catch fish!"

She grinned at him. The word play was fun. He was fun. She'd smiled and laughed more in the past few days than in her whole recent life. Guy made her feel alive again. He'd knocked the chip off her shoulder about her past and led her into the light. She put down the pole, sighed, and stretched lazily.

He watched her covetously. "A woman who likes to fish," he mused, "and who doesn't worry about getting her hands dirty."

"I like to garden, too," she remarked. "I used to plant flowers when I lived at home. Nobody does, now."

He pursed his lips and stared at the ripples on the river as it ran lazily past the banks. He was thinking about flower beds and a small house to go with them, a house just big enough for two people.

She looked up at him with soft, warm brown eyes. "I've really enjoyed being here," she said. "I'm sorry I have to leave tomorrow."

Reality came crashing down on him. He turned his head and looked at her, and saw Anita's eyes looking back at him. He blinked. "You have to leave?"

She nodded sadly. "I have to write up all these articles and get back to my desk. I expect I've got a month's work piled up there."

"In Denver."

"Yes. In Denver." She pulled in her line and put the pole down beside her. "It's been the most wonderful week I can remember. Thank you for saving my life."

He frowned. He was staring at his line, but he wasn't seeing it. "Couldn't you stay for another week?"

"I couldn't justify the time," she said miserably. "I can't just chuck my job and do what I please. I don't depend on my mother for my livelihood, you know," she added. "I work for my living."

He was more morose than he'd felt in years. He pulled in his own line and curled it around the pole. "I know how that is," he said. "I work for my living, too." He turned his head and looked down at her. He wanted to ask her to stay. He wanted to tell her what he was beginning to feel for her. But he couldn't find the words.

She saw the hesitation and wondered about it. He got to his feet and gathered the poles silently, placing them back in the truck. He glanced deliberately at his watch.

"I've got another group of cattlemen checking in at the feedlot later," he said, lifting his eyes to hers. "I'd offer you lunch, but I'm not going to have time."

She smiled. "That's okay. I enjoyed the fishing trip. Even though we didn't catch any fish," she added.

He wished he could make some humorous reply, but his heart was heavy and sad. He put out the campfire, gathered up the frying pan and the bottle of vegetable oil, and put everything in the truck.

He drove her back to the motel in silence, his whole manner preoccupied and remote.

She got out at the door to her room, hesitating with the passenger door of the truck open. "I don't guess you ever get to Denver?" she asked.

He shook his head. "Not much reason to."

"And this is the only time I've ever been to Jacobsville. I guess they won't send me back."

He searched her face and it hurt him to see the sadness in her dark eyes. He was remembering Anita again, he thought irritably, remembering how it had felt to lose her.

"It's been fun," he said with a forced smile. "I'm glad I got to know you. Keep up with that medicine," he added firmly.

"I'll take care of myself." She hesitated. "You do the same," she added gently.

He hated the concern in her eyes, the softness in her voice. He didn't want to love someone who was in such a hurry to leave him.

He leaned over and closed the door. "Have a safe trip home," he said. He threw up a hand and gunned the truck out of the parking lot.

Candy stared after him, perplexed. She'd thought they were building toward something, but he seemed anxious to get away from her. She bit her lower lip and turned to go into her room. Amazing how wrong her instincts were lately, she thought as she opened the door and went inside. She seemed to have no judgment whatsoever about men.

Guy, driving furiously back to the feedlot, was feeling something similar. He couldn't bring himself to beg her to stay, after all. If her job was so important, then who was he to stop her? Perhaps he'd been too hasty and she didn't want him on any permanent basis. That made him irritable, and the more he thought about it, the more frustrated he got.

By early evening, he was boiling mad. He had supper in the bunkhouse and then drove himself out of town to the most notorious bar in the county and proceeded to drink himself into forgetfulness.

He realized the stupidity of it, so he drank more. In no time at all he was bleary-eyed and spoiling for a fight.

Cy Parks, usually unsociable and rarely seen around town, had stopped by the joint for a beer and saw him. He had a good idea why Guy was there, and he knew just the person to do something about the situation. He walked right back out the door and drove himself to the motel where Candy was staying.

He rapped on the door with his good hand. She came to open it, still wearing jeans and a tank top, with her long hair around her shoulders. She gaped when she realized who was standing at her door.

"Mr. Parks!" she exclaimed. "Did you come to tell me something else about your operation, for the article?" she asked, voicing the most likely reason for his presence here.

He shook his head. "I phoned Justin Ballenger from my car and asked where you were staying." His black eyes glittered, and not just with impatience. He almost looked amused. "I thought you might like to know that Guy Fenton is getting tanked up at the local dive. He looks in the mood to break something. I thought you might like to try your hand at keeping him out of jail."

"Jail?" she exclaimed.

He nodded. "Rumor is that the sheriff won't give him a second chance if he wrecks the bar again."

"Oh, dear," she murmured. She sighed. "Can you drive me out there?"

He nodded again. "That's why I came."

She didn't hesitate. She all but jumped into the passenger seat of his luxury car and fastened her seat belt before he climbed in behind the wheel.

"I made him fly," she said heavily. "I had an asthma attack at the Caldwell place and he had to get me back to town in a hurry, so he had to fly Matt's plane. I brought back all the memories of the girl who died in the plane crash. Poor Guy.''

He glanced at her. ''Are you sure that's what sent him out to the bar?''

''I can't think of anything else.''

He smiled to himself. ''Justin says you told him you'll be leaving tomorrow.''

''That's right,'' she said with resignation. ''The boss only gave me a week to do these articles. I can't stay any longer.''

He didn't reply to that. But his whole look was speculative as he drove. He pulled up at the bar and switched the engine off.

''Want me to go in with you?'' he asked.

She glanced at the sheer size of him, and almost said yes. He looked tough, and she knew that having a damaged hand wouldn't save any man who challenged him. But it would be cowardly to take protection in with her, she considered.

''Thanks, but I think I'll go in by myself,'' she said.

''I'll wait out here, then,'' he replied. ''Just in case.''

She smiled. "Thanks."

She got out and walked warily into the bar. There was a hush, nothing like the regular sounds of clinking glasses and conversation and loud music. The band was sitting quietly. The customers were grouped around a pool table. As she watched, a pool cue came up and went down again and there was an ominous cracking sound, followed by a thud and a louder bump.

Following her intuition, she pushed through the crowd. Guy was leaning over a cowboy with a bleeding nose, both big fists curled, and a dangerous look on his face.

She moved right up to him, without hesitation, and caught one of his big fists in her hands.

He jerked upright and stared at her as if he was hallucinating.

"Candy?" he rasped.

She nodded. She smiled with more self-confidence than she felt. "Come on, Guy."

She tugged at his fist until it uncurled and grasped her soft hand. She smiled shyly at the fascinated audience and tugged again, so that Guy stumbled after her.

"Don't forget your hat!" a cowboy called, and sailed Guy's wide-brimmed hat toward them. Candy caught it.

There were murmurs that grew louder as they made it to the front door.

Guy took a deep breath of night air on the steps and almost keeled over. Candy got under his arm to steady him.

"My God, girl, you shouldn't...be here," he managed to say, curling his arm closer. "Anything could have happened to you in a joint like this!"

"Mr. Parks said they'd arrest you if you broke it up again," she said simply. "You rescued me. So now I'm rescuing you."

He began to chuckle. "Do tell?" he drawled. "Well, now that you've got me, what are you going to do with me?" he asked in a sensuous tone.

"If she had any sense, she'd lay a frying pan over your thick skull," Cy Parks muttered. He moved Candy out of the way and propelled Guy to the car. He shoved him headfirst into the back seat and slammed the door after him.

"We'll drop him off at the feedlot and then

I'll take you home. Justin can send somebody for the truck.''

"What are you doing here?" Guy asked belligerently. "Did she bring you?"

"Sure," Cy said sarcastically as he cranked the car and pulled it out of the parking lot onto the highway. "She drove my car to my house and tossed me in and forced me to come after you."

Guy blinked. That didn't sound quite right.

"I'm sorry I made you fly," Candy said, leaning over the back seat to look at Guy. "I know that was what did this to you."

"What, flying?" he murmured in some confusion. He pushed back sweaty hair. "Hell, no, it wasn't that."

"Then what was it?" she asked hesitantly.

"You want to go home," he said heavily. He leaned back and closed his eyes, oblivious to the rapt stare of the woman in the front seat. "You want to walk off and leave me. I had a job I was beginning to like, but if I can't have you, I have nothing worth going on for."

Cy exchanged an amused glance with a shocked Candy. "What if she stayed?" Cy asked. "What good is a man who gets stinking drunk every Saturday night?"

"If she stayed I wouldn't have any reason to get drunk every Saturday night," Guy muttered drowsily. "Could get a little house, and she could plant flowers," he murmured on a yawn. "A man would work himself to death for a woman like her. So special..."

He fell asleep.

Candy felt her heart try to climb right out of her body. "He's just drunk," she rationalized.

"It's like truth serum," Cy retorted. "So now you know." He glanced at her. "Still leaving town?"

"Are you kidding?" she asked, wide-eyed. "After a confession like that? I am not! I'm going to be his shadow until he buys me a ring!"

Cy Parks actually threw back his head and laughed.

Guy came to in a big bed that wasn't his own. He opened his eyes and there was a ceiling, but it didn't look like the ceiling in the bunkhouse. He heard soft breathing. Also not his own.

He turned his head, and there, beside him in the bed with just a sheet covering her, was a sleeping Candy Marshall. She was wearing a pink silk gown that covered only certain parts of her exquisite body, and her long dark hair was spread over the white pillow like silk.

He looked down and found that he was still wearing last night's clothing, minus his boots. He cleared his throat and his head began to throb.

"Oh, boy," he groaned when he realized what had happened. The question was, how had he gotten here, in bed with Candy?

She stirred. Her eyes opened, dark velvet, soft and amused and loving.

"What are we doing here in bed together?" he asked dazedly.

"Not much," she drawled.

He chuckled softly and grabbed his head.

"How about some aspirin and coffee?" she asked.

"How about shooting me?" he offered as an alternative.

She climbed out of the bed, graceful and sensuous, and went to plug in the coffeemaker that was provided with the room. She had cups, and she went to her purse and pulled out a bottle of aspirin. Before she shook them out, she paused to use the preventative inhalant Dr. Morris had prescribed.

"Good girl," Guy murmured huskily.

She glanced at him and smiled. "Well, I have to take care of myself so I can take care of you." She brought him the aspirin and a glass of water. "Take those," she directed. "And if you *ever* go into a bar again on Saturday night, I really will lay an iron skillet across your skull!"

"They'll arrest you for spousal abuse," he pointed out.

"Put your money where your mouth is," she challenged.

He chuckled weakly as he swallowed the aspirin. "Okay. Will you marry me, warts and all?"

"We've only known each other a week," she stated. "You might not like me when you get to know me."

"Yes, I will. Will you marry me?"

She smiled. "Sure."

He laughed with pure delight. "Care to come down here and seal the bargain?"

She hesitated. "No, I don't think so. You're in disgrace. First you can get over the hangover and clean yourself up a bit."

He sighed. "I guess I do look pretty raunchy."

She nodded. "And you still smell like a brewery. By the way, I don't drink. Never."

He held up a hand. "I've just reformed. From now on it's coffee, tea, or milk. I swear."

"Good man. In that case, we can get married next week. Before Saturday night," she added with a smile.

He opened his eyes wide and studied her with possessiveness. "It wasn't flying at all," he said softly. "It was losing you. I couldn't bear the thought that you were going to go off and leave me. But this time the alcohol didn't work. I've lost my taste for bars and temporary oblivion. If you'll marry me, I won't need temporary oblivion. I'll build you a house where you can plant flowers." His gaze dropped down over her slender body. "We can have children, if it's safe for you."

She beamed. "I'd like that."

"It might be risky."

"We'll go ask Dr. Morris," she assured him. "Since I'm going to be living in Jacobsville, he can be my doctor."

He just stared at her, his heart in his eyes. "I didn't know it could happen like this," he said aloud. "I thought love died and was buried. It isn't."

She smiled brilliantly. "I never even knew what it was. Until now."

He opened his arms and she went down into them, and they lay for a long time just holding each other tightly in the shared wonder of loving.

He lifted his head finally and looked down at the treasure in his arms. "I suppose, if you want to, I can go back to my air cargo company and run it."

"Do you want to?"

He thought about that for a minute before he answered her. "Not really," he said finally.

"It was a part of my life that I enjoyed at the time, but there will always be bad memories connected with it." He put his hand over her lips when she started to speak. "I'm not still grieving for Anita," he added quietly. "I'll always miss her a little, and regret the way she died. But I didn't bury my heart with her. I want you and a family and a home of our own. I enjoy managing the feedlot. In many ways, it's a challenge." He grinned. "And if you'd take over publicity for the local cattlemen's association, we'd have a lot more in common."

She beamed. "Would they let me?"

"They'd beg you!" he replied. "Poor old Mrs. Harrison is doing it right now, and she hates every word she writes. She'll make you cakes and pies if you'll take it off her hands."

"In that case, I might enjoy it," she replied.

"And we'd get to work together," he murmured, bending to kiss her gently. He lifted his head. "Oh, Candy, what did I ever do to deserve someone like you?" he asked huskily. "I do love you so!"

She pulled him down to her. "I love you, too."

* * *

Neither of them questioned how love could strike so suddenly. They got married and spent their honeymoon in Galveston, going for long walks on the beach and lying in each others' arms enjoying the newness of loving in every possible way.

"My mother wants us to come and visit her when we're back from our honeymoon," she mentioned to Guy after a long, sweet morning of shared ecstasy. She curled closer to him under the single sheet that covered them. "She said she hoped we'd be happy."

"We will be," he mused, stroking her long hair with a gentle hand. "Do you want to go?"

"I think it's time I made my peace with her," she replied. "Maybe I've been as guilty as she has of living in the past. Not anymore," she added, looking up at him with love brimming over in her eyes. "Marriage is fun," she said with a wicked grin.

"Is it, now?" He threw off the sheet and rolled over onto her with a chuckle. "Was that a hint?" he whispered as he began to kiss her.

She slid against him with delight and wrapped a soft long leg around his muscular one. "A blatant hint," she agreed, gasping as he touched her gently and his mouth settled on her parted lips.

"Anything to oblige," he whispered huskily.

She laughed and gasped, and then clung to him as the lazy rhythm made spirals of ecstasy ripple the length of her body. She closed her eyes and gave in to the pleasure. Love, she thought while she could, was the most indescribable of shared delights.

Outside the window, waves crashed on the beach and seagulls dived and cried in the early-morning sunlight. Somewhere on the boundary of her senses, Candy heard them, but she was so close to heaven that the sound barely registered.

When the stormy delight passed, she held an exhausted Guy to her heart and thought of flower gardens in a future that was suddenly sweet and full of joy. She closed her eyes and smiled as she dreamed.

Guy felt her body go lax. He looked down at her sleeping face with an expression that would have brought tears to her eyes. From a nightmare to this, he was thinking. Candy had made him whole again. She'd chased away the guilt of the past, and the grief, and offered him a new heart to cherish. He knew without a doubt that his drinking days were over. Candy would make his happiness, and he'd make hers.

He settled back down beside her and drew the sheet over them both. In his mind, before he fell asleep, he was already working on plans for that small house where he and Candy would share their lives.

nightmare to this, he was thinking. Candy had made him whole again. She'd chased away the guilt of the past and the grief, and given him a new heart to replace his. Even without a doubt that his waiting days were over, Candy would make new beginnings, and he'd under last.

He settled back down beside her and drew the child that went forth in his mind before he fell asleep he was already working out plans for that small house where the three of them would share their hope.

LUKE

"That best portion of a good man's life,
His little, nameless, unremembered acts
Of kindness and of love."

—William Wordsworth

Chapter 1

Luke Craig was a rancher, and he'd battled all sorts of problems over the years. He'd had to deal with falling beef prices, closed markets, crazy winters and bad fall harvests that required him to buy feed for his livestock over the winter. But the problem that had just cropped up was one he'd never seriously considered. A summer camp for underprivileged city kids had just opened right next door to his ranch, and he was having to come to terms with invaders who made the Mexican Army in 1836 look tame by comparison.

To top it all off, the owner of the camp was a feisty young woman who seemed to have cornered the market on bad temper and stubbornness. Her name was Belinda Jessup. He knew her brother, Ward, slightly, having met him at cattlemen's association meetings in the past. Ward was more interested in oil wells than cattle, as a rule, but he still kept his membership in various groups that dealt with livestock. Belinda didn't resemble her brother all that much, but they shared the same hot temper. She wasn't bad looking, with her dark blond hair and green eyes and outgoing personality. Strange how she rubbed Luke the wrong way.

His sister Elysia liked Belinda. Of course, Elysia had just married Tom Walker, the father of her young daughter Crissy, and right now, in the glow of nuptial bliss, she liked everyone. Luke, living alone for the first time in years, was heartily sick of his own cooking and his own company. Belinda's project made him even more irritable than he normally was.

It had come as a shock to discover that old man Peterson had sold the river property that adjoined Luke's to an outsider. It had been sudden, too. The land hadn't been advertised, not even with a sign on the roadside. One day, old man Peterson owned it. The next, it was being developed as a youth camp, complete with roofed pavilion, small cabins, and a pier on the river. Luke's pasture adjoined the property. It was delineated by a sturdy electrified fence and a steel farm gate with a padlock. The very first morning Ms. Jessup's city kids came to stay, the padlock was skillfully removed and the gate opened. Neighbors had called the sheriff's office to complain that Luke's Hereford steers were roaming the neighborhood— and the highway.

Luke and his men had rounded up the cattle, put them back into the fenced pasture, and the padlock had been replaced by a chain half the size of one that held a ship's anchor, affixed with eight combination locks.

The next morning, the sheriff's deputy was back with the same complaint about loose cattle. Luke checked and all eight combination locks were lying on the grass, rusting.

It was inevitable that the rancher would go straight to the source of the problem.

Belinda was working out the next day's recreation schedule when she heard the sound of a horse's hooves outside the large cabin that served as her main office. She'd heard about the liberated cattle and she had a cold feeling that retribution was at hand.

She went out to meet trouble head-on. It was trouble, too; a lean, lithe man in denims and wearing an expensive wide-brimmed hat and hand-tooled boots with silver spurs that even her brother would have coveted.

As he came closer, she saw that he was incredibly handsome, with thick blond hair and eyes as blue as a china plate. He had a firm mouth and a square jaw, and an expression on his lean face that could have curdled milk. She didn't need telling that this was Luke Craig. She'd already heard about him in town, although most people said he was easygoing and friendly. He didn't seem that way to Belinda.

She held up both hands. "We're quite willing to pay damages," she said at once. "I know who the culprit is, and I've had words with him. Strong words."

He put both hands on his narrow hips and glared down at her. It was a long way down, too. She was a little woman. "If those had been my breeding bulls instead of steers, we wouldn't be having words, Miss Jessup," he said in a deep, cutting tone. "You'd be locked up in the county jail, alongside your larcenous cohort."

"My larcenous…!" Her mouth closed with a snap. "You hold it right there, cowboy," she said shortly, losing patience and diplomacy in one breath. "These kids have never had much. They live in abject poverty with parents who don't want them. Some of them have been beaten, some have been addicted to alcohol and drugs, some have been in jail. The oldest is barely seventeen, and I'll leave you to imagine the sort of upbringing they've had. I opened this camp to give them a glimpse of life as it could be, as it should be! I brought them here to learn that there's more to the world than dirty houses and drunk parents and the sound of gunshots every night they live."

He studied her with open curiosity, his expression giving away nothing of his thoughts. "You're a one-woman salvation society, I gather."

"Actually, I'm a poorly paid public defender in Houston," she replied. "In the sum-

mer, I take a few kids camping. This year I
decided to buy some land and make it a permanent camp.''

He nodded. "Right next to my largest pasture.''

"This is Texas,'' she reminded him.
"You've got lots of room. I only want this
little tiny bit of land, right here, that I bought
and paid for.''

"You didn't pay for the right to let my cattle
loose.''

She sighed heavily. "You're right, I
didn't,'' she admitted. "And if I hadn't insisted on bringing Kells along with me, you
wouldn't have been inconvenienced twice in
one week. I'm sorry.''

She'd piqued his curiosity. He'd known several do-gooders, but most of them were all talk
and no action. "Kells?''

"The seventeen-year-old,'' she continued.
"I defended him when he was arrested for
shoplifting. Last month I convinced the judge
to give him a second chance and asked for him
to be remanded into my custody from juvenile
hall.'' She grimaced. "He's not your ordinary
slum kid. There hasn't been a lock built that

he can't pick. If they put him in prison, he'll be a master safecracker by the time he gets out, complete with diploma.''

''Having learned the trade from pros, in the slammer,'' he agreed.

''Exactly.'' She searched his blue eyes curiously. ''Socially conscious, are you?''

''I watch the six o'clock news,'' he returned. ''And I'm all for prison reform. I just don't want it next door to me.''

''That's how everyone feels,'' she told him. ''It's the same with any unpleasant thing. Yes, let's have a new sanitary landfill, but not on land adjoining mine. Yes, let's have an incinerator, a water treatment plant, a new factory— but not on land adjoining mine.''

''You can't blame people for guarding their investments,'' he pointed out. ''And I work as hard for my income as you work for yours, Miss Jessup.''

She smiled. ''I know a little about cattle. My brother's into oil exploration these days, but he still runs a thousand head of Santa Gertrudis on his ranch up in Ravine.''

''He's from Oklahoma originally, isn't he?''

''No, but our mother was,'' she corrected.

"We still have relatives there," she murmured, without adding that they never had any
contact with those relatives, or their scandal-
ous mother, who'd deserted them to run off
with a married man.

"I know your brother," he added unexpectedly. "I go to a few cattlemen's conventions,
when I can manage time. He got married a few
years ago, didn't he?"

"Yes, to one of the few women in the world
he actually likes," she murmured dryly. She
looked past him at the big black-spotted white
horse he was riding. "Nice mare."

"She's four," he said with a smile. "An
Appaloosa. I breed a few of them."

"My boys would love to ride a horse," she
murmured.

His face hardened. "Would they? There's a
riding stable a mile down the road—Stan's
Bar-K Ranch."

"I know. I've already approached him about
riding lessons," she said with a smug grin at
his chagrin. "Spiked your guns, huh, Mr.
Craig?"

He looked around at the cabins. Curtains
moved in one. He'd have bet money it was the

boy she'd mentioned—Kells. He glared toward the spot and the curtain fell together and remained still.

"Nice glare," she murmured. "How long did it take you to perfect that?"

"All my life." He pulled the hat farther over his eyes and glared down at her. "No more opened gates. I'm putting a man out here on night duty. A city policeman. He'll be armed."

She drew her breath in sharply. "You'd have him shoot a child for trespassing?"

"I would not," he said coldly. "But I'm trying to make you see the seriousness of the situation. It wasn't so many years ago that leaving a gate open could get you hung in Texas."

"So could insulting a lady," she drawled.

He lifted a blond eyebrow and a corner of his mouth tugged up in a very sarcastic smile.

She actually blushed. Her hands clenched at her sides. "I'll be sure and tell Kells that your storm trooper is lying in wait for him."

"Some storm trooper," he murmured. "A family man with six kids and ten grandkids who can't make it on what they pay him to risk his life every shift he works.''

She had the grace to feel ashamed. ''Sorry.''

''You've been standing on the wrong side of the law for a while, haven't you?'' he asked coolly. ''Perhaps you should spend a little time with the victims of the people you defend and broaden your view of the world around you.''

Her indrawn breath was audible, even above the brisk wind in the trees around them. ''That was uncalled for! You have no idea what I do—''

He cut her right off. ''I have every idea! I sat in court and watched an ambitious public defender accuse my mother of asking to be beaten every night of her life by a drunken lunatic who caused her to miscarry two children.'' His blue eyes blazed in a face gone taut with horrible memories. His fists clenched at his sides. ''To hear him tell it, my father was a victim of his family, not the reverse. Well, sadly for him, there were color photographs of my mother and my sister, very graphic ones, that the jury got to see.'' The hatred he felt for the whole legal system was written all over him as he spoke in curt, deep tones laced with bitterness. "They put him away for five years, despite all the legal chicanery and smooth talk, but not in time to save my mother. She'd suffered so much abuse that years were taken off her life. She died right after he was convicted."

She was shocked that a total stranger would tell her such a thing about his family. She was more shocked that he made her feel dirty with his confession, and vaguely guilty as well.

"I'm sorry," she said with genuine sympathy.

"Sorry." He looked her up and down coldly. His eyes went past her to the cabins. "Yes, you're sorry for the way the legal system works, Miss Jessup. So sorry in fact that you've brought a few future lawbreakers down here to the brush, to coddle and baby them so that they're even more convinced that society owes them a living for the horrible bad lives they've lived." He glared at her. "I could write you a book on dysfunctional families and physical abuse, but I've never picked a lock or stolen a car or shot another person in my life, except during Desert Storm when my army reserve unit was called up."

She moved back a step. "I'm not trying to defend criminals, Mr. Craig. I'm trying to turn some potential criminals around before they become the real thing."

"Pamper them, then," he mused. "And see how long it takes one of them to slit your throat while you sleep." He leaned forward. "But don't take my word for it," he added sardonically. "It's been my experience that stubborn people have to learn the hard way."

"You have a very narrow view of life," she replied.

He looked down his nose at her. He knew he was being harsh, but something about her egged him on. "I'll bet you were loved and wanted and spoiled, weren't you?" he asked.

She was unnerved by that blue glitter. "My childhood is none of your business."

He laughed hollowly. "To hear you tell it, every criminal's childhood is my business. Poor little murderers and thieves and rapists. They just needed a little more love to be good citizens. And the people they victimized probably deserved it, didn't they?"

She was shocked. "I never said that!"

"You do-gooders think it. They said my mother asked to be beaten."

She winced. "Of course she didn't!"

"Really? The public defender was eloquent about that. He had dozens of reasons why she enjoyed having her face broken time and time again."

"He was doing his job," she said. "Even the worst criminal has the right to an attorney."

"Of course," he drawled. "And every public defender has the right to build a reputation for setting the guilty free."

"Was your father set free?" she asked pointedly.

"The public defender convinced the parole board to let him loose early," he told her. "He'd have come back with blood in his eye and taken his rage out on my sister and me. But he dropped dead in his cell of a heart attack. I suppose God still believes in justice, even if the legal system has forgotten the meaning of the word." He turned around. "I won't have the boy shot if he picks that lock again. I will have him arrested and prosecuted." He paused, glancing back at her. "I'm not a poor country kid at the mercy of the system now. I can afford the legal help of my choosing, and pay for it. If I lose any more cattle, you won't be taking one of your charges back to the city after summer camp. And that's the only warning you'll get.''

He swung back into the saddle, turned the horse, and rode back the way he'd come, his back as straight as a board.

Belinda watched him go with more conflicting emotions than she'd felt in her life. He was a bitter man, and they'd made an enemy of him because Kells couldn't keep his fingers to himself. If she wasn't careful, if she didn't keep a close watch on the boy, she'd land him in jail herself, when her whole purpose in coming here was to keep him and his mates out of trouble.

She worried the thought all through the evening meal of hot dogs and French fries, her green eyes on the lanky dark youth with the curly black hair who sat idly at the table taking a pocket watch apart and putting it back together for amusement.

Kells was hard to reach. He was ultrasensitive about his lack of grace and looks as well as his background. He had five brothers and sisters scattered around the country with various relatives. He'd moved here with his mother and her boyfriend, but the boyfriend didn't want him and his mother wouldn't fight for him. He'd stolen a CD player on purpose to get back at her when her boyfriend had beaten him. In his neighborhood, many people had criminal records. But Kells had magic in his fingers and something in his manner that set him apart from his peers. Belinda had recognized the potential in him. She believed in him. She was the only person who did. She'd had to fight his mother and the whole juvenile court system to get him here to summer camp. Now he was seventeen and he could go to jail if he was arrested. She might have taken him out of the frying pan only to land him in a fire.

He noticed her scrutiny and his black eyes came up, hostile and faintly defensive. "I can put it back together," he muttered when he saw her eyes on the watch.

"I know you can," she said, and smiled. "You're very clever with your hands, Kells. I don't think I've ever known anyone your age who had the facility you have with mechanical things.''

He averted his eyes and shrugged, but she sensed that the compliment had pleased him. ''That cowboy going to arrest me?''

''He's a rancher. It was his cattle you turned loose, twice.''

''I never turned no cattle loose,'' he said with his head down.

''You picked his locks and opened the gate. The cattle turned themselves loose.''

He made a jerky motion with his head. ''Never seen cows before,'' he mumbled.

''Steers,'' she corrected.

His eyes came up and he seemed suddenly alert. ''Steers? What's the difference?''

''Cows are mothers of calves. Heifers are unbred cows. Bulls are stud cattle. Steers are neutered cattle raised for beef. Those were steers. They're beef cattle.''

His whole face seemed entranced. ''Like at the supermarket, ground beef and all.''

She smiled. ''Yes, that's right.''

He lost interest in the watch. ''Why does he keep them apart from the others?''

''Bulls won't tolerate a steer, and mother

cows will fight them to protect their calves,'' she explained. ''Besides that, it's logistics. It's easier to have different categories of cattle in a bunch, easier to work them when it comes time to separate them.''

He leaned forward. ''Work them?''

She chuckled. ''During roundup. You have roundup twice a year on the ranch, once in the spring when the calves come and once in the fall, when you're rounding them up for sale or culling nonproducers. Calves have to be dehorned, branded, given their vaccinations, castrated if they're to be beef cattle, and tagged.''

He was really interested. His eyes were more alert than she'd ever seen them. ''Do they have names or something?''

''They have numbers, usually on their ear tags, but sometimes they're tattooed or a computer chip with the individual animal's history is implanted under the hide to be read with a scanner.''

''You're kidding!''

''I'm not. We still have rustlers in the cattle industry, even today.''

''Did those steers have computer chips?''

"I don't know." She pursed her lips. "We could ask Mr. Craig."

He grimaced. "Oh, he won't talk to me," he said. "I know how people are around here."

She studied him quietly. "How are they?"

"Prejudiced," he muttered.

She smiled. "Did you know that a quarter of all the cowboys in the west during the last century were black?"

"They were?"

"African Americans and Hispanic Americans still make up a good portion of the numbers out here on ranches—they certainly do on my brother's. And I'm sure you've heard about the Ninth and Tenth Cavalry—the Buffalo Soldiers—and the Fifty-sixth and Fifty-seventh Infantry units. All African American."

"You mean, the Buffalo Soldiers were *all* black?"

She nodded. "They had the highest reenlistment rate and the lowest desertion rate of any group in the army."

He seemed to grow taller as she spoke. "They didn't say nothing about that in history class."

"It's changing," she said. "Slowly but surely American history is starting to include contributions by all races, not just the whites."

His lips tugged into a reluctant smile as his long-fingered hands toyed with the watch. "You're okay, Miss Jessup."

"So are you, Kells. Don't worry about Mr. Craig. Everything's going to be fine."

"I don't know," he said quietly. "It's not hard to see that he don't want us here."

"Sure he does," she countered. "He just doesn't know it yet!"

Chapter 2

Luke was fuming when he got home. He hated the whole idea of his new neighbors. It wasn't bad enough that the largest part of his hay crop had been ruined by too much rain, or that cattle prices were falling after a bacteria scare. Some days it didn't pay to be a rancher. He wondered why he hadn't gone into some better paying profession, like plumbing. It was sheer lunacy to hang on to a ranch, even if it had been in the family for three generations.

He tossed his hat onto the sofa and sat down in his big recliner to watch the news. There was a feature on about the rise of juvenile crime and the lack of proper punishment in the juvenile justice system. He laughed without mirth. The same old tired theme again, and now he had a better knowledge of juvenile crime than most people. He'd put the eight combination locks back on the farm gate between his pasture and the summer camp, and he'd talked to his friend in the police department about working two nights a week out there.

He allowed himself a moment to ponder the trespasser's future if he'd left a gate open on the other side of that summer camp, on land that belonged to Cy Parks. Luke was fairly easygoing, even in a temper. Cy Parks was so bad-tempered that delivery boys had to have double pay just to take things out to his place. Luke had considered talking to him about the summer camp, because there was safety in numbers. But he decided against it. Cy was a newcomer to Jacobsville and he'd never made any attempt to get to know local people. Rumor had it that he'd been burned out on his Wyoming ranch and had barely escaped with his life. He'd bought old man Sanders's place

on Verde Creek and was building a herd of
purebred Santa Gertrudis cattle. If Kells had
so much as sneezed on one of those expensive
young bulls, there was no telling what Cy
would do. Luke, of course, was a kindhearted
man. That being the case, he had to resort to
desperate measures to protect his cattle. So he
planned to hire a watchman.

His property contained a little line cabin
near the fence, which Luke had furnished with
a stove and refrigerator, chairs, a table and a
cot for the men when they were working out
there during roundup. It was a good few miles
from the ranch proper, and he didn't run a
chuck wagon to roundup, so the cabin was
largely self-sufficient. There was a kitchen, so
the men could cook for themselves, and the
small building even had a telephone. Luke
would provide his security man with a pair of
binoculars, special ones with infrared, so that
they allowed night vision. He wasn't going to
lose any more cattle through open fences. No
matter what it took.

The next morning, on a day when he was
going to install the security man in the line

cabin, he rode out to the steer pasture to find the gate closed. But the steers weren't alone in the pasture. A tall, lanky dark youth was stalking one of the steers.

Luke spurred his mount, something he rarely ever did, and put on a burst of speed, insinuating the horse in front of the boy, who backed away with huge wide eyes and upraised hands.

"Get that thing away from me!" the boy yelled. "Don't let it kick me!"

The fear in the youth's face was a surprise. Luke reined in the horse and sat quietly, leaning slightly forward in the saddle to study the nervous youth on the ground.

"What the hell are you doing in my pasture?" Luke demanded in a cold tone.

"Looking...looking for them computer chips," Kells stammered.

It was the very last thing Luke had expected to hear. He sat hesitating, his mind working furiously.

He wasn't aware of Belinda's cry or her headlong rush over the locked gate, so frenzied that she almost ripped a hole in her elegant designer jeans and scarred her boots.

"It's all right!" Belinda cried, panting as

she ran up to join Kells, moving just in front of him. "He wasn't doing anything to the cattle!"

"Steers," Kells corrected, feeling a little smug.

Luke looked at him with new interest. "You know something about cattle?" he asked unexpectedly.

"She was teaching me," he replied, jerking his head toward the small woman in front of him. "About the difference. You know, steers and heifers and such. And about the computer chips under the hides."

Luke's hostile expression had faded to curiosity. "She told you about that?"

He nodded. "I wanted to see the chips. I wasn't going to hurt nothing," he added with faint belligerence.

Luke actually chuckled. He abruptly rode off toward where the steers were congregating near the fence, lifting his lariat from the saddle horn. He spun a loop and lassoed one of the steers with easy grace, the result of years of long practice, and got down out of the saddle to catch the rope tight. He motioned to Kells.

"That was great!" Kells exclaimed. "That

was just great! How you learn to do that, spin that loop and lasso that cow...that steer...so easy?''

Luke grinned. ''A lot of practice and a few bruises,'' he murmured. He was petting the steer behind its ears, and the animal stood very still and looked content. ''Come on, he's not dangerous. I only run polled cattle here.''

''Polled?'' Kells asked, curious.

''Dehorned,'' the older man qualified. He searched behind the steer's neck and felt for a small lump. He found it. ''Here.'' He caught Kells's dark hand and smoothed it over the spot. ''It's a computer chip. I resisted this technology for years, but it makes roundup so much easier that I finally gave in. We can keep an animal's entire herd history on one chip and get the information in seconds with a scanner when we sort the animals for sale.''

''I didn't think ranchers used it on steers,'' Belinda interjected.

''Oh, we don't usually,'' he agreed. ''But this lot is an experiment.'' He shifted a little self-consciously. ''I've been reading about some new methods that our local cattlemen's association is using. Vasectomy, for one.''

"What's that?" Kells asked.

"Ordinarily, you create a steer by removing what makes him able to reproduce. But by giving the steer a vasectomy," he explained, "the animal still produces testosterone, which we think is responsible for fast growth. But since the steer is effectively neutered, it tends to be easier to handle. You get a higher weight-gain ratio the same as with bulls, but you get the lean carcass of a steer."

"Isn't it expensive to do it that way?" Belinda asked.

He smiled. "Not really. It takes about the same amount of time, and we do it ourselves instead of calling out the veterinarian. But even if it did take more time, we think the benefits outweigh the cost. That's why we're experimenting with it. Since the animal gains weight without the use of growth hormones, we save some money there, too."

"My brother says a lot of consumers are getting scared of those additives, like growth hormones and antibiotics," Belinda agreed.

"There's definitely a market for organically grown beef, and at least one cattleman I know of is offering custom-grown lean beef to supermarket chains,'' he added. He noted Kells's light, fascinated touch on the animal's shoulder.

''Isn't it hard to kill them?'' Kells asked unexpectedly.

''Yes,'' Luke replied unexpectedly. ''I'm in the cattle business because I like animals, so I get attached to the damned things. They all have personalities. They're all different. I try not to get too close to the beef cattle, but I've got a ton and a half bull who follows me around like a pet dog, and two Holstein milk cows who think they're cats.''

Kells chuckled. ''No fooling? What's a Holstein?''

''They're dairy cattle...look here, are you really that interested in cattle?''

Kells shrugged and lowered his gaze to the steer. ''Never saw cattle before,'' he murmured. He glanced shyly at Luke and then away again. ''I like them. I didn't mean to let them get loose. I wanted to see them up close, you know. And after she told me about the computer chips...'' He grimaced. ''I just wanted to see what it looked like.''

Luke pursed his lips, aware of Belinda's

stillness. "Want to come see the Holsteins?"
he asked.

Kells caught his breath. "You fooling?"

Luke shook his head. "Nothing a cattleman
likes better than to show off his operation."
He almost laughed aloud at the expression on
Belinda's face.

Kells was fascinated. "Reckon I could see
that bull?"

Luke chuckled. "Sure. Why not."

"Aren't you scared of that thing?" Kells
persisted, moving back from the big black-
spotted white horse.

"She's gentle—a mare," Luke explained.
He frowned. "Why are you afraid of horses?"

"I lived in New York City until this year,"
he muttered. "A cop on a horse tried to run
me down. It reared up and if I hadn't moved,
it would have pawed me."

Luke wisely didn't ask what Kells had done
to provoke the man. Still, trying to ride a boy
down, for any reason, was reprehensible.
"You should have told someone in authority,"
he said curtly.

Kells shrugged. "Nobody ever wanted to do
anything for me until my mom moved us to

Houston a few months ago and I got in trouble for taking a CD player out of a shop. She—'' he indicated Belinda ''—went to bat for me and got the owner not to press charges. But I got sent to juvy anyway, 'cause I was sixteen then.''

"Juvy?"

"Juvenile hall," Belinda told him. "Courts are harder on juveniles these days, because there's so much violence in the inner city."

"I see." He didn't. He studied Kells, who was watching the cattle with such fascination that he was drawn to the boy. All his prejudices about "coddling juvenile delinquents" were going up in smoke. It was easy to be intolerant when you didn't know the people you were intolerant toward. Kells was giving him an education in gray areas, where before he'd seen only black-and-white.

"When do you want me to bring the guys over?" Belinda asked him.

"No time like the present," he said. "Load 'em up and come on. Know how to find it?"

"Yes, I've seen it from the road," she replied. She smiled with genuine gratitude. "Thanks."

He shrugged. "Just being neighborly." He took the loop from the steer's neck and coiled the rope, with Kells watching every move. The young man had a quick mind and nimble fingers. Suddenly he had an idea that might bear consideration.

There were six kids from the ghettos of Houston in Belinda's group, ranging in age from nine to fourteen. Kells was the oldest. The youngest was Julio, a Mexican boy. Two were white and one of the others was black, like Kells. The middle boy, Juanito, was Native American, although he wouldn't say which tribe. He didn't talk about himself at all. In fact, he didn't talk much, period. He was living with an uncle and aunt who didn't seem to notice what he did, or care. It was the same story with most of the others. That's why they'd landed themselves in juvenile court and detention centers. They cared as little for themselves as the adults around them did. It was important to Belinda that someone cared about them, built their self-esteem, made them proud of their races and history. She didn't delude herself that she could change the whole world. But maybe she could change one person.

She drove the boys to Luke's ranch in the rickety old van she'd bought for the occasion. It was in good mechanical shape, even if it did look like the dark side of the moon. She thought of having it painted, but it seemed a waste of time and money.

As she reached the end of a long, winding graveled road that led off from a paved highway, she noticed Luke was waiting for them. The house was nice, big, white and friendly with a long porch. There was a stable and corral back away from the flower garden that Luke's sister had kept until her marriage, and there were fenced and cross-fenced pastures reaching all the way to the main road.

Belinda got out of the battered old van and opened the side door so the boys could get out with her. "Remember not to go through any fences, okay?" she cautioned them. "Bulls are dangerous and unpredictable. If you've ever watched rodeo, in person or on television, you'll know that already."

"Mr. Craig said his bull follows him around," Kells reminded her.

"So he does. But the bull knows Mr. Craig, doesn't he?" she replied.

Kells grinned. "I guess so."

Luke came down the steps to meet them, greeted the boys, and led them toward the barn. "This ranch has been in my family for three generations," he began. "My grandfather started out with longhorn cattle and I ended up with Herefords. Most ranchers have a breed they prefer above others. Cy Parks, who lives across there—" he gestured back toward the space the summer camp occupied "—runs purebred Santa Gertrudis. One of his bulls cost a million dollars."

Kells eyes widened and then his face fell. "Gosh, I guess you got to be rich to have cattle, huh?"

Luke smiled at him. "Not really. You could start out with a young bull and a few heifers and build a ranch from there. It's not as expensive as you think."

The light came back into the youth's eyes. He looked past Luke to the big Hereford bull in the pasture adjoining the barn and his breath caught. "Oh, Lord, what an animal!"

Luke burst out laughing. "He sounds just

like me at his age," he explained when everybody looked at him. "I thought there was nothing on earth as pretty as a bull."

"There isn't," Kells agreed. He got up on the bottom rung of the high wooden fence and wrapped his arms around the top rung. "Isn't he great?"

"His name's Shiloh," Luke told him. "I raised him from a baby and now he's mentioned in just about every major cattle journal as a top stud bull. I can't keep up with the demand for his progeny. There's even a waiting list."·

"Got any buffalo?" one of the boys asked.

Luke shook his head. "I know of a ranch or two that runs some, but they're dangerous to keep. They'll charge at the least provocation and they can go right through a fence."

"They have buffalo up on the Yellowstone," Juanito said. "I saw a whole herd when my uncle drove us through the park."

"I never saw a buffalo," another boy murmured.

Belinda smiled at her charges. "The whole of the western states used to have herds of

them, before white people came along and
killed them off.''

''Why'd they do that?'' one of the others
wanted to know.

''Greed,'' Luke said flatly. ''Pure and simple, greed. They wanted the money that people
back east and even overseas were willing to
pay for buffalo hides. And, too, there was a lot
of money to be had for guiding shooting parties out on the plains so that they could kill
hundreds of buffalo for sport and leave them
lying in the sun.''

Belinda stared at him curiously and then she
smiled. They were kindred spirits. She hated
the loss of the buffalo, too.

He glanced down at her while the boys murmured to each other about the size of that big
bull in the fenced pasture. She had a pretty
face, he thought, and a big heart to go with it.
He liked her already. He smiled slowly and
was surprised and delighted to see her face
flush.

She had to drag her eyes away from his.
That look had gone right through her. Over the
years she'd had plenty of boyfriends, but they
were all just casual acquaintances. Or they had

been until Russell, who gave her an engagement ring and swore he loved her, and then
eloped with her best friend. That had been four
long years ago. She hadn't looked at another
man since.

"What's wrong?" Luke asked perceptibly.

She caught her breath. "Wrong? Why...
nothing."

"You were thinking about something and it
hurt. What was it?"

She shifted. "I was engaged. He eloped with
my best friend."

"Well, well." He studied her carefully. "So
that's why you aren't married. No inclination
to try again, I gather."

"None at all."

"Join the club."

She shot a quick glance at his averted pro-
file. "You, too?" she asked softly.

He nodded, a jerk of his head. "Me, too. She
promised to be true, but the minute I went off
on business, she was entertaining an old boyfriend at the local motel." He laughed coldly.
"You can't do that sort of thing in a town this
small and not be gossiped about. Two people
told me about it when I got off the plane."

"It's the world we live in," she said quietly. "Fidelity doesn't seem to mean much, anymore."

He turned to face her. "It means the world to me," he said flatly. "I'm an old-fashioned man. When I give my word, I keep it."

She grimaced. "So do I." She smoothed her fingers carefully over the hard wood of the fence. "He said I was a dinosaur."

One eyebrow levered slowly up.

"I wouldn't go to bed with him because we weren't married," she said simply. "So he found somebody who would." She shrugged. "I can't blame him, really. I mean, every woman does it."

"Not every woman," he said coldly. "Virtue is so rare as to be priceless these days."

"Show me one virtuous man," she dared.

"That would be difficult," he agreed, "although it's not impossible. I've known a man or two who felt the way you do about it. Still, men can't get pregnant, can they? Women are the childbearers, the civilizers. I believe that when children are going to be involved, there should be one man, and no others."

She stared up at him quietly. "You're a dinosaur, too."

"You got a dinosaur?" one of the boys, overhearing, asked.

"Don't be stupid," another boy answered him, "there's no such thing!"

"I read that dinosaurs turned into birds," another ventured.

Juanito grinned for the first time. "My grandad used to say he could turn into a bird when he liked. And my mom said no wonder he ate like one."

Everybody laughed, but kindly.

It broke the ice. Luke showed the boys around, and they warmed to his easy, friendly manner. He led them through the barn, where he had two calves being treated for scours and a heifer with snakebite.

"They're all improving," he said, watching the boys stare at the animals. "They'll go out into the pasture in a day or two. There were three calves in here, but we lost one of them yesterday."

"What's scours?" Kells asked.

"It's a disease calves get that prevents them from keeping anything in their stomachs," he replied. "They die if they aren't treated. The vet has been giving them medicine for it. Usually it works. Sometimes, it doesn't, no matter how hard you try."

"I guess you have to use a horse to work cattle," Kells continued.

"I'm afraid so. Although," he added with a chuckle, "I used to know a man who used an all-terrain vehicle to do it."

"One of those four-wheeled things like a big lawnmower?"

"The very thing. He hit a stump unexpectedly and went headfirst, right into the lagoon. I hear he gave the vehicle to his nephew the next day and went back to using horses." He saw the question in Kells's eyes and before he could ask it he added, "A lagoon is where animal waste is collected."

Kells doubled over laughing. "No wonder he gave the thing away!" He sighed. "I guess I could learn to like horses."

"Sure you could," Luke assured him. "A horse that's trained right will do what you tell it to, although I've seen some bad horses. In fact, a neighbor of mine has a twenty-year-old horse that killed a man in an arena and was about to be destroyed. He saved it."

"Must be a nice man."

He shook his head. "Not a chance. He's like a rattlesnake, coiled up and waiting for somebody to come within striking distance." He grinned. "Most people walk wide around him."

"Can we go back out there and look at the bull?" Kells asked.

"Sure, go ahead."

They ran out almost in a unit, leaving Luke and Belinda together at the steel gate that contained the calves in their stall.

He glanced at Belinda. "That neighbor lives on the other side of your camp, by the way. You'd better make sure nobody trespasses in his direction. I'm a reasonable man. He's not."

"I'll remember," she promised.

He watched her openly, his blue eyes narrow and thorough on her soft oval face. "Do you like your job?"

"I like kids," she said. "Especially kids who need something society isn't giving them." She jerked her head toward the boys. "There's not one thing wrong with them that a little love and attention wouldn't have taken care of. They just want someone to care about them, and they find unorthodox ways to attract attention.''

"Kells said he stole a CD player."

She nodded. ''But not because he wanted it,'' she murmured. ''His mother's boyfriend had beaten him up that morning. He was getting back at her, for exposing him to that sort of treatment.'' She shrugged. ''The boyfriend is the reason they're out here. He sent for her, but he doesn't want Kells. Neither did his father.''

"What a shame."

She nodded. ''The boyfriend's idea of discipline is a fist to the jaw. I've had the D.A.'s office looking into it, but Kells's mother won't say a word in Kells's defense. In fact, she told the investigator that he asked for it, by being sassy.''

"Nobody asks to be beaten up." He said it with such ferocity that she turned and looked up at him. His face was hard, set with lines of pain. She had the most terrible urge to reach up and touch it, to make the lines relax. She remembered very well what he'd told her about his father, about the beatings. It would have been worse, to watch his mother taking that sort of abuse and not being able to stop it. It was a sadly familiar story in her circles. She reflected on women she'd worked with who had been victimized by abusive husbands.

There seemed to be so many women who tolerated the abuse out of fear, a kind of fear that well-meaning outsiders could never understand. Belinda tried to explain that everything would change once the woman was out of the house. It rarely worked until a beating landed her in the hospital, or until the man injured, sometimes killed, one of her children.

"What are you brooding about?" Luke asked abruptly.

She smiled sadly. "About women who won't accept help, feeling they're better off where they are. I was thinking about why they won't leave men who hurt them."

"Because they're afraid," Luke replied curtly. "Everybody says, just get out, you'll be okay." He laughed bitterly. "Once, after the police left, my father held a butcher knife to my mother's throat for ten minutes and described to her, graphically, what he'd do to my sister, Elysia, with it if she ever called the police again.''

"Dear Lord,'' she breathed.

"He meant it, too,'' he added. "He said he'd have nothing to lose if they were going to put him in jail anyway.''

She put out a hand and touched the back of his, just lightly. "I'm sorry you had to go through that.''

He turned his hand and caught her fingers in his, tightly. "Why did you become a public defender?''

She smiled ruefully. "My best friend was raped by her stepfather, and the public defender on her case had such a heavy workload that he plea-bargained the case to get it off his schedule. She was devastated when her stepfather didn't even have to serve time for what he'd done. She couldn't go back home, because by then her mother believed she'd invited it.'' She shook her head sadly. "I decided then and there that I wanted to make a difference in the world. I studied law and here I am, despite my brother's assurances that I was wasting my time.''

He chuckled. "I remember your brother

very well," he mused. "He was the most ruthless businessman I ever met."

"Yes, he was. His wife has changed him,"
she added. "He's given up being stone-
hearted. Now, he's my biggest fan."

His blue eyes met hers and he smiled slowly.
"Maybe, but he's not your only one." He
leaned closer deliberately, pausing with his
lips a breath away from hers. "I like you, too,
Miss Public Defender." And then he kissed
her.

Chapter 3

He'd meant it to be a brief, teasing kiss. It didn't work out that way. The touch of that soft mouth under his was explosive. He caught his breath, lifting his head just enough to see the mutual shock and pleasure in Belinda's eyes before he bent again.

This time, it wasn't brief, or particularly gentle. He lifted her completely against the length of his tall, muscular body and kissed her until he had to come up for air. He looked into her stunned eyes with quiet curiosity, breathing raggedly.

"You should...put me down," she whispered.

"Are you sure?" he murmured while he searched her face.

"Yes. The boys..."

He eased her back onto her feet, shooting a glance toward the barn door. The youngsters weren't in view at all. "Nobody saw," he said. He traced her swollen lips with his forefinger. "I could get used to this," he added quietly. "How about you?"

She swallowed and then swallowed again. She had to move back from contact with him before her mind would work again. "I'm only here on my summer vacation," she managed in a voice that didn't sound like her own.

He smiled slowly. "Houston isn't that far away."

She didn't know what to say. She was overcome by feelings she'd suppressed, tucked away and forgotten. Her body felt like a rosebud subjected to rain and sun and wind, blooming and lifting its face to the elements. He was very attractive, and he had qualities that she loved. But it was too quick; too soon.

"I'm rushing you," he mused, seeing the

confused uncertainty in her eyes. "Don't get uptight. I won't back you into a corner. But I'm interested. Aren't you?"

She took time to catch her breath. She lowered her eyes to his shirt. "Yes."

He grinned. His heart felt lighter than it had in years. He curled her fingers into his and led her toward the barn entrance. "Come on. I'll show you my horses."

Belinda went along silently. She couldn't believe he'd done that, right out in the open, in plain daylight. It had been a passionate kiss, deliciously arousing and hungry. The warm, hard contact left her confused and quiet.

He had several horses, all Appaloosas. He explained the markings and called their names. "I'm crazy about them," he remarked. "I belong to an Appaloosa club and we talk on the internet about our passion. This is one special breed."

"Everybody says that about whichever breed they like best," she said with a laughing smile. "But I can see why you like Apps. They really are beautiful."

"Cy Parks has Arabians," he told her. "A small herd, with a glorious stallion herd sire.

He's pure white, like beach sand on the Gulf of Mexico. I think he used to race them, before he moved here.''

"Is he really such a rough customer?''

"Yes, he is,'' he said bluntly. "Keep your brood well shy of his ranch. He can't tolerate children at all,'' he added, without mentioning why.

She let out a soft whistle. "Thanks for the warning,'' she said. "I started this camp because I wanted to make a difference for these boys, if they could see another sort of life from the one they live in the inner city. Yet I never stopped to consider the potential pitfalls... Still, I'm encouraged by Kells's interest in ranching. He didn't seem the kind of teenager who'd fall in love with cattle so quickly, but he's genuine about it. This will give him something to work toward.''

"I had an idea about that,'' Luke confided. "I thought I might ask him to stay at the ranch and learn the ropes while you take the others back to your camp. Then if he decided to come back here and work after graduation, I'd hire him.''

She caught her breath. "You'd do that for him?"

"For myself, too," he said. "He's a quick study and he loves the business. A cowboy like that would be an asset anywhere. If I train him, I can hire him when he gets through school."

"He'd be over the moon."

"Don't tell him until we can get the details worked out," he cautioned. "I don't want to build him up to a big letdown."

"I won't say a word." She searched his face. "You're good with children."

"I learned on Elysia's little girl," he told her with a grin. "I took her to movies and the park and carnivals. Her dad does those things now. I've missed her since Elysia remarried."

She studied the Appaloosas. "You should get married and have kids of your own."

"You know, I've just realized that."

She didn't dare look at him. Her heart was leaping around madly in her chest.

He turned away from the horse pasture and tugged her along with him. "We'd better get back to the boys and make sure they aren't trying to climb aboard that old bull," he murmured dryly. "I still remember how I was as a kid."

"How did your father make a living?"

"My grandfather made the living for him," he replied. "He had this ranch. Dad worked for him, when he was sober enough, and my grandfather protected us as long as he was alive. When he died, everything changed."

"But you managed to hang on to the ranch."

"I had help," he said. "Neighbors, friends, relatives…everybody did what they could for us, despite my father. That's why I'm still here," he added seriously. "Jacobsville is the sort of place where you're not a resident, you're part of a family. Maybe people know your business, but they care about you as well. I couldn't think of living anywhere else."

"I can understand why," she murmured. Her hand in his felt small and vulnerable. *She* felt small. He towered over her, and she liked him very much. Too much. It wasn't possible to feel so strongly for someone she'd only just met, but she seemed to fit into his life as if she'd been conditioned to it.

He glanced down at her with a warm smile. She was pretty and feisty and she really did care about these boys of hers. He could see her with children of her own. She'd be a veritable mama lion if her kids were threatened. He found himself wondering about having a child of his own. He loved Elysia's two, but he had to start thinking about the future, about kids of his own to inherit this place when he was gone. It didn't really surprise him that he was beginning to see Belinda in a new light. She came from a ranching background, and she had a soft heart. He'd had his fill of women who wanted a good time and no ties of any kind. He was old enough to start looking for a settle-down sort of woman.

The boys left the ranch late that afternoon with Belinda, after a long tour of the ranch on saddle horses that left them all sore but happy. "They'll be uncomfortable tomorrow," Luke chuckled as he saw Belinda to the van. "They used muscles they didn't know they had on that trail ride. Kells took to it like a pro, did you notice? For a boy who was afraid of horses, he's come a long way in a short time."

"You were amazing with him," she said.

"He was the one I couldn't reach, did you know? He was surly and uncommunicative until I started telling him about cattle. I found the door and you found the key. He's different."

"He's focused," he told her, glancing toward the van where the boys were conversing animatedly inside. "They're not bad kids," he said suddenly, as if the thought surprised him.

She smiled. "No, they're not," she replied. "The world is full of them. Young people get married and two years down the road, they realize they've made a mistake, but they've got a child. They get divorced and marry somebody else and the kids end up in a family where they're the outsiders. Sometimes they're not even wanted. It's worse in poor neighborhoods, of course." She nodded toward the van. "Kells could write a book on that. He said that most of the kids in his neighborhood in New York City were either wanted by the law or selling drugs. He thought he'd end up the same way." She sighed, her eyes seeing far away. "When people live in hopeless poverty, with a poor self-image and no way out, they give up. That's why they resort to alcohol and drugs, because it eases the pain, just for a little

while. But pretty soon, they're hooked and
they can't quit, and they'll do anything to get
high again, so they can forget where they live
and what they've become." She shook her
head. "It occurs to me sometimes that a small
percentage of people aren't constructed to live
in a regimented, money-oriented, time-clock-
mandated industrial society. These same people, placed on the land where they could work
at their own pace, would be happy and use-
ful."

"That's a new theory."

She shook her head. "It's not. I'm only
quoting Toffler." He looked puzzled and she
smiled. "Alvin Toffler...*Future Shock?* Mr.
Toffler is a visionary and he sees right inside
people. He said that some people will never fit
into our fast-paced culture, and I think he's
right."

"I'd like to hear more about that." He
pursed his lips. "I don't suppose you could get
away for supper one evening?"

"I've got no one to stay with the boys," she
said regretfully.

"Then I'll just have to find an excuse to

have them back over again, won't I?'' he said, grinning down at her.

She chuckled. ''You do that. I'd better get them back to camp. Thanks for letting me bring them over.''

''I enjoyed it,'' he returned.

''So did I.''

She went back to the van and climbed in with the boys. She couldn't help a glance into the rearview mirror as they went back the way they'd come, down the winding ranch road. Luke was standing in the yard with his hands in the pockets of his jeans, his wide-brimmed hat covering his head. He looked like part of the land itself, and something warm kindled inside her at just the sight of him.

For the next few days, Belinda found plenty of time to regret her lapse of control with Luke in the barn. She got cold feet and flatly refused the boys' request for another visit to the ranch.

She didn't realize that her refusal was about to have grave consequences. Kells, depressed with little to do and too much time on his hands, wanted another shot at roping cattle.

Late one sunny afternoon, he slipped away

from the others. He'd found an old, limp rope
in one of the old outbuildings near the camp
and he'd spent hours every day practicing with
it, as he'd seen Luke do. He was somewhat
proficient, but he was bored with roping the
old sawhorse that sat near the oak tree behind
the building. He wondered if he could lasso a
steer. Miss Jessup was occupied with the other
boys, teaching them how to use her laptop
computer. He preferred cattle to computers, so
he coiled his rope and sneaked down the road
toward a pasture full of red-coated cattle.

He didn't realize that Luke's cattle were
only one side of the long, winding graveled
road. He knew that most of Luke's steers were
Herefords, which were white and red. These
cattle were red, but they might be a variation
on the same breed, he decided. They sure
weren't steers, he knew that by looking at
them, and they had horns. They'd be easy to
rope! He slipped through the barbed-wire
fence stealthily, eased into the small line of
trees that outlined the green pasture, and
started up a small rise where a red-coated
young bull was grazing.

It was the perfect time to practice the lariat

throw he'd been perfecting, as Luke had showed him how to do it. He missed the first time he tried, but the animal didn't run away. It stood chewing grass and staring at him curiously. He coiled the rope and patiently tried again. This time, he managed the throw perfectly, tossing the loop right over the short horns of the young bull. He chuckled and let out a whoop as he started reeling the bull in.

He was having the time of his life, leading the young bull around the pasture and down the hill toward the gate when he heard a loud yell, followed by a chilling report that sounded very much like a rifle being fired.

He stopped dead in his tracks, the rope in his hand, and turned to find a tall, threatening-looking man on a huge white horse sitting just a few hundred feet away on the ridge holding a rifle to his shoulder. His face wasn't visible under the wide-brimmed hat, but the threat in his posture was immediately recognizable to a teen who'd had several brushes with gangs.

Kells dropped the rope and threw up his hands while he had time. "I was just practicing with the rope, mister," he called. "No need to shoot me!"

The man didn't reply. He had a cell phone in his hand now and he was punching in numbers. A minute later he spoke into it and then closed it up.

"Sit down," a rough, deep voice called.

Kells wasn't thrilled with the idea of sitting down in a cow pasture where rattlesnakes might be crawling, but he didn't want to get shot. He sat down. This, he thought, was very obviously the landowner Luke had warned him about, but he hadn't listened. He knew with a miserable certainty that he was going to wish he had.

Belinda was just beginning to clear the lunch dishes and wondering why Kells hadn't come in to eat when her cell phone rang. She picked it up and listened, and then sat down hard.

"They didn't have your number, so they called me," Luke told her grimly. "If you'll give me a minute to organize things here, I'll pick you up and we'll go to the police station together. I know these people better than you do."

"What are my chances of getting Mr. Parks

to drop the charges?'' she asked with resignation in her voice.

"Slim to none," he said flatly. "If Cy Parks had his way, they'd probably shoot him. I don't think we'll be able to talk Cy out of this, but we can try."

"How long will it take you to get over here?" she asked, not even protesting his offer to go with her.

"Twenty minutes."

Actually, he made it in fifteen. He was dressed for work, in wide leather bat-wing chaps, old boots with caked spurs, and a long-sleeved chambray shirt. He pulled his wide-brimmed hat farther over his eyes as he put Belinda into the huge double-wheeled pickup truck and drove her into town.

"Don't get the idea that our police department is gung-ho to arrest people for no good reason," he said as he drove. "Cy will have bulldozed them into it. By the letter of the law, Kells was trespassing, but nobody in his right mind would take a rustling charge seriously. What was he going to do with the damned bull, anyway?"

"He was practicing with the lariat, the way you taught him," she said miserably. "I suppose he got tired of lassoing the sawhorse and wanted something real to practice on."

"He heard me tell him to keep off Parks's place!"

"He wouldn't have known which side of the fence was Parks's," she returned. "He probably wasn't even paying attention to the color of the animals. At any rate, yours have red-and-white coats and Parks's have red coats, he might have thought some of yours were a solid color."

"It's a hell of a mess, I'll tell you that," he said angrily.

"Worse than you know. With his record, he may never get a chance to go home again. They'll want to send him right back to the detention center and keep him there."

"Damn!"

She felt furious at Cy Parks for this. Kells shouldn't have been on his property, but he was a kid, and he didn't think. Why did Parks have to abide by the very letter of the law?

It seemed forever before Luke pulled up in front of the neat brick building that contained the police and fire departments and the city jail.

"In here," he indicated, holding the door open for Belinda.

The building was air-conditioned and very neat. Luke opened the door that had Police written on it, and ushered her to the counter, behind which a clerk sat.

"We're here to see about bail for the Kells boy," Luke said.

"Ah, yes." The clerk took a slow breath and sorted through papers, shaking her head. "Mr. Parks was furious." She glanced at Luke. "He's still here, you know, giving the chief hell."

Luke's blue eyes turned to steel. "Is he, now? Which way?"

The clerk hesitated. "Now, Luke..."

"Tell me, Sally."

"He's in his office. I have to announce you."

"I'll announce myself," he said shortly, and forged ahead, leaving a startled Belinda to follow him.

This was a side of Luke that she hadn't seen before. He barged right into Chief Blake's of-

fice with only a preemptory knock, and found
the chief looking uncomfortable while a tall,
whipcord lean man with venomous light green
eyes and jet-black hair raged at him.

Cy Parks turned as Luke entered the office,
his lean face as unwelcoming as a brushfire.
"I won't drop the charges," he said at once,
narrow-eyed and threatening. "I don't want juvenile delinquents camped on my south pasture, and I'll have every damned boy on the
place in jail if that's what it takes to keep them
out of my cattle!"

"That sounds familiar," Belinda said under
her breath.

Luke wasn't intimidated. He walked right up
to Cy, almost on eye-level with the man, and
pushed his hat back on his blond hair. "I
taught Kells to use a rope," he said angrily.
"He's crazy about roping. He's been practicing on my cattle, but they don't have horns."

Cy didn't speak. But he was listening.

"He's an inner-city kid who got arrested for
swiping a CD player. He didn't want the ap-
pliance, he wanted to get back at his mother
for letting his stepfather beat him up."

Cy's stiff stance relaxed just a little.

Encouraged, Luke plowed ahead. "He's not a juvenile now, so if you press charges, they'll lock him up for good. He'll never get out of the justice system. He'll become a career criminal in between terms in prison, and I'll lose the most promising young cowhand who's ever come my way."

Parks's eyes narrowed. "He likes cattle?"

"He's obsessed with cattle," Luke replied. "He's drained Belinda dry and now he's starting to pick my brain. He has a natural seat on a horse. He eats, sleeps, and breathes cattle since he's learned how to tell one breed from another."

Parks's jaw clenched. "I don't like kids around me."

Luke didn't blink. He noticed that Cy always kept his left hand in his pocket, and he knew why. The man hated sympathy; it was probably why he was so mean. It kept most people at bay. "Hating kids isn't going to bring yours back," Luke said quietly.

The other man's face clenched. He stiffened and for an instant, it looked as if he might throw a punch at Luke.

"Go ahead," Luke invited softly, evenly.

"Punch me if you feel like it. I'll give you a free shot. But let the kid go. The last thing on earth he meant to do was damage any of your stock. He loves cattle."

Cy's fist balled by his side and then relaxed. He moved his shoulders, as if they felt stiff, and glared at the other man. "Don't mention my past again," he said in a tone that chilled. He glanced at the police chief. "If I drop the charges, do you let him go?"

"With a warning," Chief Blake agreed.

Cy hesitated. He turned toward Belinda Jessup, who was pale and quiet and obviously upset. "What was the idea behind this summer camp?" he asked curtly.

"I brought six inner-city kids to the country to see what life could be like," she replied calmly. "Most of them have never seen a cow, or a pasture, or a small town. They grew up in poverty, with parents who didn't really want them, and all they saw were people working themselves to death for minimum wage or men in luxury cars dealing drugs for big money. I thought, I hoped, that this might make a difference." She folded her hands behind her. "It was making a major difference in Kells, until now. I'm sorry. I should have been watching him more carefully. He's spent two days practicing with the rope. I suppose he thought he was in Luke's pasture when he roped the bull.''

"Hell of a difference between a purebred Santa Gert and one of those damned mangy Herefords," Cy said curtly.

"Hey," Luke said testily, "don't insult my Herefords!"

They glared at each other again.

"What about Kells?" Belinda interjected before things escalated too far.

"Let him go," Cy said shortly.

Chief Blake smiled faintly. "I'm glad you decided that," he said, rising. "I never thought roping a bull should be a capital crime."

"You haven't seen my new Santa Gert sire," Cy returned.

Blake just chuckled and went to the back to bring out Kells.

Kells was chastised and miserable, and looked as if the world had ended. He grimaced when he saw Cy Parks standing there.

"I guess I'm going back to Houston, now,

huh?'' he asked Belinda with overly bright eyes.

"No, you're not," Luke said curtly, glaring at Cy. "You're coming over to the bunkhouse at my place for the rest of your camp leave."

Kells looked as if he'd been knocked sideways. "You're kidding, right?"

"I'm not," Luke assured him. "If you want to rope cattle, you have to be around them. Besides, we've got to talk about the future. Your future," he added. "Let's go."

Kells hesitated. He walked up to Cy Parks and bit his lip while he searched for the right words. "Look, I'm sorry about what I did, okay?" he asked hesitantly. "I knew them cattle didn't look exactly like Mr. Craig's, but I thought he might have had some more, and that was them. I never meant no harm. I just wanted something alive to practice on. Ain't no challenge in roping a few boards nailed together."

Cy looked uncomfortable. He made a strange gesture with his right hand. "All right. Don't do it again."

"I won't," Kells promised. "Them bulls sure are pretty, though," he added with a shy smile. "That breed started on the King Ranch in South Texas, didn't it?"

Cy's lower jaw fell a little. "Well, yes."

"Thought so," Kells said proudly. He smiled. "I'll know next time how to tell a Santa Gertrudis from a Hereford."

Cy exchanged a complicated glance with Luke. "I guess you could bring him over to see my new Santa Gertrudis bull," he said gruffly. "Call first."

Luke and the other occupants of the room gaped at him.

Cy glared back. "Are you all deaf?" he asked irritably. "I'm going home. I don't have time to stand around and gossip all day, like some I could name." He tipped his hat at Belinda in an oddly old-world gesture, and stormed out the door.

Kells caught his breath as the rancher lifted his left hand out of the pocket to open the door, but Cy, fortunately, was out the door before it was audible.

"What happened to his hand?" he exclaimed.

"His Wyoming ranch burned up in a fire," Luke said quietly. "His wife and young son were in the house at the time. He couldn't get them out. Not for lack of trying, that's how he got burned.''

"Oh, boy," Kells said heavily. "No wonder he hates kids. Reminds him of the one he lost, don't you think, Miss Jessup?''

She put an affectionate arm around Kells. ''Yes, I do. Poor man. Well, let's get back. I left the others at lunch.''

"Sorry about all the trouble," Kells said.

Luke grinned at him. "It was no trouble." He glanced at the chief of police and smiled. "Thanks, Chet.''

Chet Blake shrugged. "All in a day's work. I was trying to get him to drop the charges when you walked in. But I didn't get far, I'm sad to say. I couldn't budge him.''

"He's a hard-nosed fellow," Luke agreed. "But he did the right thing in the end.''

"So he did. Maybe he's not frozen clean through just yet," Blake replied.

They drove back to Belinda's camp in a companionable silence.

"I'm taking Kells with me," he told her when he pulled up in front of the cabin, and the boys piled out onto the porch to greet Belinda. "I'll get him settled and you can come over in a couple of days and check on him."

"I thought you were kidding!" Kells exclaimed. "You meant it?"

"Of course I meant it," Luke told him. "You're a natural cowboy, Kells. I'm going to make you into a top hand. Then, when you get through school if you're still of the same mind, I'll take you on as a cowboy."

Kells could hardly speak. He stared down at his hands in his lap and averted his head. There were bright lights in those dark eyes until he blinked them away. His voice was still choked when he said, "Thanks, Mr. Craig."

"Luke," he corrected. "And you're welcome."

"Have fun," Belinda told Kells.

He got into the front seat beside Luke and closed the door, leaning out the open window to wave to his friends. "I'm going off to learn cowboying, you guys! See you!"

They waved back. Belinda joined them on the porch and waved the truck off with a grin.

"Is Kells going to jail?" Juanito asked.

"No, he isn't. Mr. Parks dropped the

charges," she said with heartfelt relief. "In a day or so, we'll drop by the Craig ranch and see how Kells is doing. But for now," she added with a groan as she saw the disorder of the small kitchen and dining-room table, "we're going to have a dishwashing and housecleaning lesson."

The groans were audible even outside the cabin.

Chapter 4

Belinda kept busy with the remaining boys in her small group for the next two days, taking them swimming and fishing. They were like prisoners set free, with plenty of time to enjoy the natural world around them, and no regulations and time schedules penning them in. It was more than a vacation for them; it was a glimpse into another world. With any luck at all, it would sustain them when they had to go home, give them goals to work toward, give them hope.

Two days after Kells's run-in with the law,

they piled into the van and went over to Luke's ranch to see how the eldest of the group was making out.

They hardly recognized him. He was wearing new boots, jeans and chaps, a long-sleeved shirt and a raunchy-looking hat. He grinned at them from the corral fence, displaying blazing white teeth.

"Hey!" he called. He jumped down and went to meet them. "Miss Jessup, I rode a horse all morning and Mr. Craig even let me cut out a steer and lasso it! That's a quarter horse," he informed the other boys knowledgeably, nodding toward the horse in the corral. "His name's Bandy and he's a cutting horse. He's trained to cut cattle, so you don't have to do much work except sit in the saddle and let him do everything. He's one smart horse!"

"Well, he certainly thinks he is," Luke interrupted, joining the group. "What do you think of my new hand?" he asked Belinda, indicating Kells. "Looks the part, doesn't he?"

"Yes, he does," Belinda said, smiling. "We need a photo of him dressed like that," she added.

"I took one this morning," he replied smugly. "He'll have some interesting photos to show the folks back in Houston."

"I'm going to work hard, Miss Jessup," Kells said solemnly. "Harder than I ever did before. Now that I got something to look forward to, school won't be so bad."

"I'll tell you a secret, Kells," Luke told him, "school was hard for me, too. But I got through, and so will you."

"My real name's Ed," Kells said quietly. "Never told nobody else."

Luke smiled. "Is that what you want me to call you?"

Kells hesitated. "How about Eddie? I like Eddie Murphy, you know."

"I like Eddie Murphy myself," Luke replied with a grin. "I've never missed one of his movies yet."

"Son of a gun!" Kells was impressed.

"I actually saw him once," Belinda volunteered, "down in Cancun, Mexico, on holiday. He's just as nice in person as he seems to be on the screen."

"Did you talk to him?" Kells asked.

She shook her head. "I was too shy."

Luke pushed his hat back on his head and studied her with a keen, searching look. "Shy, hmm?"

She gave him a hard look. "Yes, shy! I do get shy from time to time!"

He looked pointedly at her mouth. "Do you, now?"

She flushed. "Do you think we could see those Holstein milk cows you mentioned the other day?"

"Sure we could!" Luke said at once. "Kells, suppose you take the boys along to the pasture and explain why we like to keep Holsteins for milk cows?"

The youth beamed. "I'd be tickled, Mr. Craig! Come on, guys. I know my way around here now!"

The group, impressed, followed Kells.

"Why can't I go, too?" Belinda asked.

"Because I have plans for you, Miss Jessup," he drawled. He caught her hand in his and led her toward the white frame house.

"What sort of plans?" she asked suspiciously.

He paused with a secretive grin. "What do you think?" He leaned closer, threatening her mouth with his, so that when he spoke she felt his clean, minty breath on her lips. "Well, I could be thinking about how big and soft the sofa in the living room is," he murmured. "And how well two people would fit on it."

She could barely breathe. Her heart was thumping madly against her rib cage.

"Or," he added, lifting his head, "I might have something purely innocent in mind. Why not come with me and find out?"

He tugged at her hand and she fell into step beside him, just when she'd told herself she wasn't about to do that.

He led her up the steps and into the house. It was cool and airy, with light colored furniture and sedate throw rugs. There were plain white priscilla curtains at the windows, and the kitchen was spacious and furnished in white and yellow.

"It's very nice," she said involuntarily, turning around to look at her surroundings.

"Can you cook?" he asked.

"A few things," she replied. "I'm not really good at sweets, but I can make rolls and biscuits from scratch."

"So can I, when I set my mind to it," he

told her. He sat down at the kitchen table and crossed his legs across one of the other chairs. "Can you make coffee?"

"The best," she returned, smiling.

"Let's see."

He pointed her toward the cabinet where the coffee, filters, and drip coffeemaker were located, and sat back to watch her work.

"There's a chocolate pound cake in the cake keeper, there," he indicated a huge rubbery container. "If you like it. My sister brought it over yesterday. She always bribes me when she wants something," he added on a chuckle.

"What did she want?"

"A baby-sitter," he replied. "I get to keep her son and daughter when she and Tom go to the opera at the Met in New York City. It's an overnight trip."

"You really must like kids," she observed.

"I like them more as I get older," he said. "I find I think more about having some of my own. After all, the ranch has to have somebody to inherit it after I'm gone."

"What if your children don't like ranching?"

He grimaced. "Horrid thought."

"Some people don't like animals. I've actually met a few."

"So have I. Not many."

"It could happen, though. Then what would become of your plans for a dynasty?"

"I suppose they'd go up in smoke." He dropped his hat on the floor beside his chair and stared at her until it became uncomfortable. The sound of the coffee dripping grew louder and louder in the tense silence. "Come here."

She just stood and stared at him, confused.

His blue eyes were glittery. There was a look on his face that made her knees weak. He was hypnotizing her.

"I said, come here," he repeated softly, his voice almost a sensual purr.

She walked to him, feeling every step all the way to her heart. This was stupid. She could get in over her head. She didn't really know him at all. She was letting herself be drawn in...

He reached up and pulled her down onto his lap. Before she could utter the confused thoughts rattling around in her mind, he had her head back against his shoulder and he was kissing her as if his life depended on it.

She gave in to the inevitable. He was strong and warm, and everything female in her responded to him. She hadn't realized how close two people could become in a relatively short period of time.

His arms contracted. Then, all at once, he let her go and stood up. His face was harder than she'd ever seen it. He held her tight by the upper arms, staring down into her green eyes with a curious expression.

"I think we should give the coffee time to finish," he said huskily. "Let's go find the boys."

"Okay."

She followed him back out the door, noticing the economy of his movements as he scooped up his hat and put it back on his head. He went a little ahead of her, keeping some distance between them. She felt uneasy, and she wondered if she'd been too acquiescent to suit him. Perhaps she should have hit him or protested or something. Obviously she'd done something wrong.

He opened the screen door and she started

through it, only to be encased by his long arm as it shot out in front of her, blocking her way.

"I loved it," he said gruffly. "But we have to go slow. I don't do one-night stands any more than you do."

"Oh." She seemed to have developed a one-syllable vocabulary in the time she'd known him. She kept her eyes on his arm, instead of his face.

He tilted her face up to his. "If I wanted to give you the brush-off, I'd come right out and say so," he remarked. He bent and brushed his mouth gently over hers. "You don't gulp down an exotic dessert," he whispered. "You take your time and savor it, draw it out, make it last." He nibbled her lower lip gently before he lifted his head. "Suppose I come up to Houston after you get through with summer camp? We could go to the theater and the ballet, even a rodeo if you like. I'm pretty flexible in my entertainment, I like everything."

"So do I," she said, sounding breathless. "I love opera."

"Another plus," he mused, grinning. "We'll fly up to New York with Tom and Elysia one day and go to the Met."

"I've only been there once," she told him.
"I loved it."

"It's unforgettable," he agreed. "The settings and special effects are every bit as enjoyable as the opera itself."

She shyly traced a pattern on his shirt. "I'd like to go out with you."

"Then it's a date." He glanced past her at the boys in the distance, standing in a group as if they were being lectured. Probably they were, he thought, because Kells was a quick study and he'd learned a lot in the past few days. "It wouldn't be very easy to go out even to a movie with that bunch in tow," he added with a chuckle. "They'd hog the popcorn."

"I suppose they would." She touched his arm, where the muscle was thickest and enjoyed its strength. She liked the way it felt to be close to him. "You've been good to them, especially to Kells."

"He's had a raw deal. I guess they all have, but it shows more on him. Do you know, the guys in the bunkhouse took to him right away. One of them told me that it was flattering to have a teenager ask for information instead of trying to give it. He made them feel important by asking them things." He pursed his lips. "I wonder if he realizes what a gift he has for making people like him? Even Cy Parks, who hates just about everybody."

"He's learning that he has traits he can exploit, I think. But I don't know that he would have arrived at this point so soon if you hadn't intervened. Thank you."

He shrugged off her gratitude. "Like I said, I'll benefit from all his enthusiasm. He really loves cattle."

She searched his lean face. "So do you, I think."

He grinned. "There was never anything I wanted to be more than a cowboy when I was a kid. One of our wranglers had been a rodeo star. I used to sit and listen to him by the hour."

"We had one of those, too, on my brother's ranch," she replied. "Ward and I liked him a lot, until he had an affair with our mother."

He frowned. "What?"

She sighed. "You might as well know. Our mother was very promiscuous. Anything in pants would do. She finally ran off with one of her conquests and we had to stay and live down her reputation. Ravine is about the size of Jacobsville, so you can imagine the gossip. It was harder on Ward than on me.''

"There are a lot of miserable kids in the world," he remarked.

"I noticed."

"Is that why you don't spend much time at your brother's ranch?"

She chuckled. "No. It's because of his housekeeper—excuse me, now his aunt-in-law. Lillian is a matchmaker. She brought her niece Marianne out to Texas from Georgia on some gosh-awful pretext and Ward fell in love with her. He didn't want to, so things got bad before he admitted he couldn't live without her. She's changed him. He isn't the same hard-hearted, ruthless man he used to be since he married Marianne. So Lillian had that great success and now she's got her eye on me.'' She smiled. "I don't like her choice of suitors, so I keep well clear of the ranch."

"What sort does she toss your way?"

"Big, husky mechanics and any delivery boy who comes within half a mile of the house.''

His eyebrows arched. "You're not that desperate."

"Thank you," she replied. "How about writing and telling her so?"

He grinned. "Give me time. I'll take care of that problem for you, in the most natural sort of way."

She wondered what he meant, but she wasn't confident enough to ask. She smiled and went past him out the door.

In the days that followed, Luke was almost a constant visitor to the camp. Sometimes he brought Kells, sometimes he came alone. He taught the boys how to make a fire from scratch, how to trap game, how to live off the land.

"They say these are outdated skills," he told the group after he'd started a small fire. "But what if the oil suddenly gives out and everything electronic or electrical goes dead one day? Frozen food would spoil. Computers wouldn't work. Since most telephone exchanges are computerized, communications would be out. Cars wouldn't go far, houses wouldn't have heat, air-conditioning wouldn't work. If all the old skills of survival are lost, one day the only humans who live may be the ones who can live off the land—assuming there's any land left after the developers get through.''

The Native American boy, Juanito, touched a tiny bunch of twigs that Luke had bunched to use on the tiny fire. ''My great-uncle says the same thing,'' he volunteered. ''But he can trap game and find water in places where it usually isn't. He knows which cactus plants can give water or be eaten, and he knows how to make smokeless fires. His grandfather rode with Geronimo.''

The other boys were impressed. ''But even if you can do those things, what good are they in the city?'' one of the other boys asked. ''What are you going to trap in Houston?''

''Girls,'' one of the older boys said with a wicked grin.

''He's got a point,'' Luke said, nodding toward the boy who'd asked about country skills in the city. ''People who live in cities are going to be the hardest hit if we ever have a major energy crisis. Look what happened during the last big power outage in the west.''

"They had a movie about that. It was scary," another boy said.

"Well, we've got lots of dead dinosaurs lying around yet to be discovered, so I don't think it's going to be an immediate problem," Belinda mused.

That led to the obvious question of what did dead dinosaurs have to do with energy, and for several minutes she traced the evolution of petroleum products for the boys while Luke watched and listened attentively.

Later, when the boys were in for the night and he was ready to go back to his ranch, he paused with her in the shadows, beside the pickup truck.

"You make a good lecturer," he commented.

"Thanks," she said, surprised. "Some would say I have a big mouth and can't keep it shut."

He took her hand and drew it to his chest. "I like the way you treat the boys," he said quietly. "You never talk down to them or make them feel stupid when they ask questions."

"I try not to," she agreed. "I've had it done to me in school, and I didn't like it."

"Neither did I." He smoothed his thumb over her short, neat fingernails. "You have nice hands."

"So do you." She liked the strength of them, the way her heart jumped when they touched her own hands. She looked up at him through the darkness, trying to see his face in the dim light from the cabin behind her.

He chuckled. "I was just thinking how strange life is," he told her. "I was hopping mad when I found out some lunatic was going to open a summer camp for delinquent boys right on my boundary line."

"I remember," she chuckled.

"It was a surprising day all around, especially that Kells." He shook his head. "What a treasure he turned out to be. And your guy Juanito, whose grandfather rode with Geronimo. These boys are interesting, and they aren't at all what I pictured them as."

"These are unique," she said. "But for every success, I've had three failures," she added sadly. "When I started working in the public defender's office, I had the idea that all these boys were in trouble because of their home lives. It was a mistake. Any number of them had loving parents and an extended family that really cared about them, but they could never see anything criminal about stealing and lying and hurting people. One of my charges actually wrestled me down in my office and tried to rape me.''

She felt him stiffen. "What did you do?''

"Oh, I'm an old hand at self-defense,'' she said, making light of the terror she'd felt. "I got an opening and almost made a eunuch of him. It taught me a lesson. Some of the juveniles can't be turned around, no matter how dedicated you are to saving them. There's always going to be a percentage who feel comfortable with making a living outside the law.''

"I don't like the idea that you might be attacked,'' he said.

She smiled. "I'm glad. But I'm not as naïve as I was. I never have closed-door sessions with any of my clients anymore. I have a good secretary and she's always there when I need her.'' She sighed. "But there are times when I feel so useless. Like with Kells in the chief of police's office. I really don't know what I

would have done if you hadn't been able to get
through to Mr. Parks.''

"Cy's not so bad," he said. "You just have
to stand up to him. He's the sort of man who'll
be hell on anybody who's afraid of him.''

"You weren't.''

He shrugged. "I grew up swinging," he
mused. "I learned early that fear is the worst
enemy. Once I got past that, I wasn't afraid of
much.''

"I noticed." She leaned close and laid her
cheek against his chest, feeling his arms come
around her with a sense of wonder. She closed
her eyes and let him hold her, drinking in the
sounds of the night and the warm, safe strength
of his body. "I only have a week left here.''

She felt him stiffen. His hands stilled on her
back. "A week?''

"Yes. I have cases waiting and my vacation's almost over.''

"I didn't realize it was that close.''

Her eyes opened and she saw the faint light
of the horizon far away. Crickets were chirping
madly in the night. "I've been enjoying this
so much that I didn't want to spoil it," she
confessed.

His arms tightened around her. "So have I. But I've already told you that Houston isn't that far away."

"Of course it isn't."

They both knew it wasn't quite true. It was a great distance, and Luke couldn't leave his ranch to run itself. A long-distance romance was going to be difficult, even though they both knew it was what they were leading up to.

"I don't suppose you might like to come and work in Jacobsville?" he asked.

She hesitated. "That would be nice," she said. She wondered why the thought made her so uncomfortable. He was asking for more than a move on her part, and it frightened her. He was thinking about a future that included both of them, but all she could think about was the disaster of her parents' marriage. Ward had made it work with his Marianne, but Belinda had been on her own for a long time. She wasn't ready to think about spending her life with anyone.

"We have a juvenile court system here," he continued. "It's on a circuit, and we may not have the caseload you do in Houston, but you'd stay busy. We've got local kids who could use a good attorney.''

''There are kids everywhere like that,'' she said tightly. ''But Houston is home to me now. It's where my job is. I wouldn't feel comfortable starting all over again in a new town, especially a small town.''

He was still for a moment and then he eased her away and stepped back. ''The job is that important to you, is it?''

She felt a coolness in him that hadn't been there before. But she wasn't backing down now. She was fighting for her independence. ''Well...yes, it is. I feel that I'm beginning to do some good.''

''Is your job more important than marriage would be?''

She wouldn't think that far ahead. ''I haven't thought much about marriage. Or if I have, it's a long way in the future. I don't want to be tied down just yet.''

He studied her with pursed lips and a calculating stare. ''Then you might be in the market for an affair.''

It was like a stone between the eyes. She

couldn't even find the words to express what she was feeling.

"No, I...I don't want an affair," she stammered. "I don't have time for that sort of thing. I have a caseload that's more than enough for three people, but there's only me to do it."

He let go of her completely and stood away, leaning against the hood of the truck to study her. "One thing I learned early is that jobs don't matter as much as people," he said coolly. "I've never put work before my family."

"Ward always did," she replied.

"You're not your brother. And you said he'd changed since his marriage."

"Yes, but I grew up learning that you gave everything in you to whatever job you were doing. My father hammered the work ethic into both of us from childhood."

"You don't think you could change?"

She frowned. The conversation was going far out of bounds. She wasn't sure what she believed anymore. She was drawn to Luke, but he was talking as if he wanted her to give up her job and just stay at home all the time. She

knew she could never do that. Her work was
fulfilling, important, almost sacred. She had a
mission in life that she couldn't sacrifice for
dirty dishes and housework.

"I'm not cut out to be a happy home-
maker," she said on a hollow laugh.

"No pots and pans and dirty diapers for you,
right?"

She wasn't sure about that, but he was being
sarcastic. "Maybe so," she said after a minute.
"I'm doing an important job, and it isn't one
that everybody can do. I enjoy my work. I have
to feel that I'm contributing something to the
world."

He turned his head and stared toward the
horizon without speaking. He hadn't counted
on this. He was falling in love, and he'd
thought she was, too. But she obviously wasn't
the marrying sort of woman, and she didn't
want an affair. That left nothing but friendship,
and that wouldn't be enough for him.

"I've never been much on glorious causes,"
he said finally. "I raise cattle. It's what I enjoy, and it makes a good living for me. But I
always thought that it would come naturally to
me to be a family man. I want kids. I'd be

good to them, and they'd have all the things I
didn't have when I was growing up, like loving
parents and security.'' He shrugged. ''I suppose it's an old-fashioned ideal in this modern
world, but it's still what I want most.'' He
stared off into space, his chin lifted, the air
cooling his face. He sighed and turned and
looked down at her. ''Well, I've enjoyed having you and the boys around, despite our bad
beginning,'' he said, and actually smiled.
''And if you come back next summer, you can
bring your brood over again and I'll show
them what ranching is all about.''

He was pleasant and friendly and all at once
she felt a door closing. He was going to be her
friend, her good neighbor in the summer, and
not one thing more. She knew without a word
being spoken that there would be no trip to the
opera, no weekend visits to Houston. She knew
it as certainly as if he'd spoken aloud.

''I'll remember,'' she replied in a subdued
tone. ''Thank you.''

He shrugged. ''What are friends for?'' he
mused. ''Well, I'd better be going. Keep an
eye on Kells for me when you get home, will

you? He's a fine young man. I'd hate for him to backslide.''

"I'll make sure he doesn't," she promised.

He nodded. "So long, then.''

"So long.''

She watched him climb into the cab of the truck, crank it, and drive off with a careless wave. It was more than a door closing. It was the end of something that would have been sweet and fulfilling, and she'd smashed it with a few cold words.

She folded her arms around her chest and wondered why she'd felt compelled to say things that she didn't really even believe. She was afraid, she decided. Afraid to take a chance so risky, to get married and end up as her poor father and mother had. She wasn't the sort to be unfaithful and she didn't think Luke was, either, but she'd seen a bad marriage first-hand and she was frightened.

Her job was safe, comfortable, secure. She knew where it would take her, she knew the path well. Marriage was a trek through a maze, with false turns and sudden stops and danger all around. She barely knew Luke. What if the man she saw on the surface wasn't the real man at all?

She turned around and went back inside. It was useless to speculate. She felt empty and alone, but she knew it was for the best. She was too uncertain to take that final step with Luke. He deserved someone who knew what they wanted.

Chapter 5

Belinda stuck to her guns about being independent, but if she expected Luke to try to change her mind, she was disappointed. He came by frequently to talk to the boys, and he was making inroads into teaching Kells cowboying. He brought the youth over to see Belinda, and he was open and friendly as he had been at the beginning. But he wasn't approachable.

"I guess you're packing already," he remarked a few days before her vacation ended as he stood leaning back against one of the support posts on the cabin's front porch. "Eager to get going?"

"Not terribly," she said carefully. "It's been educational and a lot of fun. But I've got work to catch up. Vacations can't last forever."

"They wouldn't be much fun if they did," he remarked. His blue eyes slid over her slender body in jeans and a knit shirt. "How old are you?" he asked abruptly.

She blinked, surprised. "I'm twenty-seven," she said.

His eyes narrowed. "The older you get, the harder it's going to be to give up your independence. You'll draw into a shell and never come back out."

She glared at him. "It's my shell."

"Pity to waste your youth on a job, no matter how important it is," he commented. "Plenty of women juggle marriage and a career and even children. It isn't impossible, especially with a partner who's willing to compromise."

"I don't want to compromise," she said stubbornly. Her green eyes flashed. "I told you, I'm happy as I am."

"Got a cat?"

She frowned. "What do I need with a cat?"

"For companionship," he emphasized. "You can't go on living completely alone. You'll get lonesome."

"I hate cats!"

"Liar."

She sighed angrily. "Okay, I don't hate cats, but I haven't got time to take care of a pet."

"You could get one of those Japanese electronic things that you have to feed and clean up after," he suggested.

"I don't want an electronic pet."

"I've got one on my computer," he drawled playfully. "It barks and growls and romps across the screen. Some of them even evolve."

"Wonderful. Just what I need. A dog to guard my computer."

"They're cute."

She hated the way her eyes kept going to his long legs and slim hips and broad chest. He was sexy and she was going overboard about him. She couldn't backslide now, when she was so close to getting away from him in time!

"Next thing you know, they'll have a life-size electronic pet that you have to feed and water and clean up after. What's wrong with the real thing?''

"Beats me, darlin'," he murmured softly, and chuckled when she flushed at the endearment. "You're the one who doesn't want to get married."

"Why should I need an electronic pet just because I don't want to get married?"

He smiled slowly. "You'd have something to lavish affection on. Something to keep you company. Something to cuddle."

"I'd like to see you cuddle an electronic blob!"

He shifted suddenly away from the post and stopped just a few inches away from her, his hands on his slim hips as he searched her flushed face. "I'd like to cuddle you, Belinda," he said softly. "We could sit on the sofa and watch TV together in the evenings when we were through with work. We could lie in my hammock on lazy summer evenings and kiss each other to a cricket and hound dog serenade. We could share coffee and cake at two in the morning when we couldn't get to sleep. Can you do that with a virtual pet or a legal pad?"

She hated what her heart was doing inside her chest. Her wide, worried eyes met his. "I'm scared!" she burst out.

"I know you are, and I know why." He touched her cheek with his fingertips, tracing a pattern on its flushed softness. "I'm uneasy, too. It's a big step from friendship to intimacy. But we've got a lot in common, and I don't mean just cattle." His fingers fell to her soft mouth. "Don't throw it away on a job."

She drew back as if his fingers scalded her. Her eyes were wide, her face drawn with misgivings and confusion. "I don't want to... belong...to anyone," she bit off. "If I stay by myself, depend on myself, I won't ever get hurt."

"Maybe not," he agreed. "But you'll never know what it is to really share love, either. You've got a big heart. You've given your time, your hard work, your heart to these boys in your camp. Why is it so hard to do the same thing with a man?"

She grimaced. "Love doesn't last," she groaned.

"It does," he disagreed. "If you can compromise, it does. Nothing comes with a money-back guarantee in this life, but people with kind hearts and things in common don't usually end up in divorce court. Try looking around you at elderly couples, people who've been together for fifty years or more. I believe love can last, if you give it a chance.''

She sighed wearily. ''I don't believe it,'' she said. ''I'm sorry. For me, that's a fairy tale. There aren't any happy endings.''

''You cynic,'' he chided. ''Take a chance. Dare everything. Risk it all.''

''I'm not a gambler,'' she replied. ''I'm a conventional, conservative woman with no real sense of adventure. I don't take chances, ever.''

He shook his head sadly. ''Well, it's a waste,'' he told her. ''You've got so much to give, Belinda. But you're wrapped up in your own fears.''

''I'm not afraid of anything!'' she flashed.

''Except love.''

She started to argue, but she couldn't find the right words.

He tapped her nose with his forefinger and smiled. ''You may be a quitter. I'm not. Just keep running, darlin'. When you've worn yourself out, I'll still be here.''

"Why?" she asked, almost in anguish.

His face sobered, and his eyes began to glitter in his lean face. "You're worth fighting for, didn't you know? And I'm a stubborn man when I want something that badly."

"It's just physical attraction!" she muttered.

"Nope."

"I'm something different, something out of the ordinary."

"You're that," he agreed. He tilted her chin and dropped a brief, hard kiss on her soft mouth. "Okay, no hard sell. But don't make the mistake of thinking I'll go away. I'm like a rubber ball. I keep bouncing back."

"I won't change my mind," she said through her teeth.

He only laughed, got back into his truck and drove off.

"I won't!" she yelled after him.

It wasn't until she realized the boys were all staring at her that she turned around and went back into the cabin.

* * *

The next couple of days passed all too quickly, not only for Belinda but for Kells. He was almost in tears when he climbed into the van for the long drive back to Houston. The boys from the bunkhouse had come out en masse to shake hands and wish him well.

"See you back here next summer, young feller," one of the older men said jauntily. "Mind you keep well shy of trouble, too!"

"Yes, sir, I sure will," Kells promised with a sad smile. "Sure am gonna miss you guys."

"We'll miss you, too, son," another wrangler agreed. "Study hard, now. Cowboying is more complicated than it used to be. You need a good education even to keep tally books!"

"I'll remember," Kells promised.

Luke was standing beside the driver's side, where Belinda was trying to be cheerful and failing miserably. She looked up into eyes that were as blue as a robin's egg and felt her heart contract painfully. He was friendly and cheerful, but suddenly remote, as if he felt nothing passionate for her at all.

His attitude confused and even wounded her, but she tried to behave nonchalantly. She held out her hand. "Thanks for all the help," she said with a forced smile. "I'd never have gotten through this without you."

He glanced at the boys and smiled and waved to them as they climbed aboard. "You had a good group. Like I said, if you come again next summer…"

"I…don't think I will," she said, having made that painful decision the night before. She didn't want to see Luke again, ever. "I'm going to put the land on the market. If you're quick, you can get it before Mr. Parks does."

He was staring at her. "I thought you'd decided that the camp was a good idea."

She shook her head. "Too many unexpected pitfalls," she replied. "If you hadn't been around, Kells would have gone to jail. I had no idea what I was getting into, although it turned out better than I expected." She stared at his top shirt button instead of his face. "I've decided to leave the special camps to people who know what they're doing. I came close to causing a disaster, with the best intentions in the world."

"Funny. I thought you did a grand job," he said.

She smiled halfheartedly. "We'll have to wait and see about that."

He pursed his lips. "I guess you're glad to be leaving," he said carelessly.

She hesitated. She almost said that she felt empty and alone, more so than ever before in her life, and that she wasn't glad at all. But the moment passed. "Yes," she said with a faint smile. "I'll be glad to get back to work." She held out her hand. "Thanks again."

He took her hand and curled his fingers into hers, watching her breath catch at the contact. She felt something for him, something powerful, he knew she did. But she was frightened and ready to bolt. He could tell by the coolness of her fingers, the uncertain flicker of her eyelids as she tried and failed to meet his eyes.

"There are no great rewards without great risks," he said under his breath.

She lifted her eyes and had them trapped by soft blue ones. "My parents…"

"You're not your parents," he replied simply. "And I'm not mine. Life is a risk. Everything's a risk. If you never take a chance, if you always try to play it safe, what's life worth? You get nothing except monotony."

"I don't like taking chances," she said curtly.

"You could learn to like it," he mused. "But you'll have to find that out the hard way, I expect."

"It's my choice," she said doggedly. "You can't tell me how to live my life."

"I can't, hmm?"

"That's right, you can't," she said firmly. "I'm leaving now. I'm going back to my own life, to my job."

"And that's all you need to be happy, right?"

"Right!" She straightened. "I'm glad you finally understand that."

He smiled in a strange, calculating way. "I understand more than you think. Well, since you're determined to leave, here's something to take back to Houston and your perfect job with you."

He moved forward and swept her up against him, bent her back over his arm in the best Hollywood tradition, and with a wicked laugh, kissed the breath and the fight right out of her. She felt as if she was melting right down the front of him, her lips hungry and aching as he kissed them, her body throbbing at the long, hard contact with his strength. By the time he was through with her, she was clinging and moaning helplessly. He had to lift her arms away and steady her before she could stand alone.

Several hectic seconds later, she wobbled to the van and climbed in, fumbling the key into the ignition to the amused catcalls of her passengers.

"I bet he watches them old movies on TV," Kells said gleefully.

"Could you be quiet?" Belinda asked. "We've got to get on the road. Goodbye, Mr. Craig!" she said gruffly.

He swept off his hat and bowed mockingly. "Au revoir, Miss Jessup!" he called after her.

She stomped too hard on the accelerator and almost flooded the engine. As the van jerked its way out of the yard toward the gates, Luke was laughing wickedly. He was a keen fisherman, and this was the championship tournament of his life. He was going to land that feisty little fish. It would take patience and fortitude, but he'd never been lacking in those qualities.

He put his hat back on and went toward the barn, whistling all the way.

The first two weeks Belinda was back at work in Houston, she felt a new emptiness in her life. She hadn't considered how lonely it was going to be without the boys. Over the weeks, she'd gotten used to them. Now, she felt as if she'd left her family behind. And she missed Luke ridiculously.

She was just leaving the courthouse after a particularly rough morning when she almost ran into Kells at the bottom of the steps.

He grinned. "I got something to show you," he said, producing a handful of papers.

She took them, looked at them, and gasped. "Why, Kells, this is extraordinary!"

It was, too. He had straight *A*'s on English, math, and science papers.

He was still grinning. "They think I'm going crazy at home, cause all I do is study. I just ignore them when they start drinking. I stay in my room and crack those books. It's not so hard, after all, Miss Jessup. You just got to get motivated."

"That's exactly right. Oh, I'm so proud of you!" she exclaimed.

He looked sheepish. "Thanks. Reckon you might tell Mr. Craig?"

She closed up. "I haven't heard from him."

"You could write him, though, couldn't you?" he persisted.

She had to agree that she could, although she didn't really want to. She sighed. "I suppose I could, considering what a happy surprise those grades are going to be for him. I'll do it."

"Thanks, Miss Jessup. And not only for that, but for believing in me," he added solemnly. "Nobody else ever thought I was worth their time."

"You're worth my time," she said with a smile. "Mr. Craig believes in you, too."

"That's what keeps me going," he told her. "That job next summer. I'm going to work so hard, Miss Jessup. I'm going to learn all I can before I go back. I'll make Mr. Craig proud of me."

"Indeed you will," she said.

"Gotta go. I'm taking a night course in Spanish," he added, surprising her. "They speak it on the ranch, you know, and there's a couple of Mexican hands. See you, Miss Jessup!''

She waved and then caught her breath at his ambition. To think that only a few short months ago, he might have ended up in juvenile hall for good, and then in jail. How many children like Kells never made it because they had no one to encourage and believe in them? She felt good inside. If she only pulled one child out of the hopelessness of poverty, her job was worthwhile. Why couldn't that hardnosed cowboy in Jacobsville understand that, she thought furiously.

Then she remembered that he'd asked how she'd feel about working in Jacobsville, and what she'd told him. She'd said that she couldn't do such a job anywhere except Houston, and that was baloney. Of course she could. But she was frightened. She didn't want to fall in love and get married. She wanted to depend on one person, herself. She couldn't imagine risking her heart.

She went on down the street to her car, feeling despondent and miserable. If only she'd never met Luke Craig!

* * *

It wasn't easy to ignore Kells's request about that letter to Luke. In the end, Belinda was all but forced by her conscience to send him a note. It was friendly, not too intimate, and factual. It took her twenty tries before she had the right words. She mailed it and waited.

But the reply didn't come in the way she expected. After a particularly long session in court with a client, she dragged herself up the steps to her apartment and found a familiar face leaning against the wall near her door. He was wearing a navy suit with a tie, and he looked more sophisticated than any rancher she'd ever known.

"Luke!" she exclaimed.

He chuckled and scooped her up in his arms, kissing her hungrily right there in the hall. Her raincoat, her valise, her pocketbook were scattered like grains of corn while she kissed him back. It was only then that she realized how much she'd missed him.

"No need to ask if you missed me," he murmured before he kissed her again. "How about supper?"

"I'm famished," she said breathlessly. "But I don't have anything to cook..."

"There's a nice restaurant down the street. I've made reservations," he said. "Put your gear inside and freshen up."

She was reluctant to take her arms from around his neck, and she laughed at her own feelings. "It's good to see you," she said, trying to act normally as she paused to scoop her stuff from the floor.

"It's good to see you, too," he replied with a smile. "You look worn."

"It's been a long week." She searched his eyes before she put her key in the lock and opened the door. "It's been a long several weeks," she added honestly.

"I know."

She put her things in a chair and turned to him. He looked tired, too. He was devastating to a heart that had gone hungry for the sight of him. For several seconds, she just stood there and looked at him.

He did the same. In her beige dress and high heels, with her dark blond hair in soft waves down to her collar, she looked lovely.

"If you want supper at all," he said huskily, "you've got ten seconds to stop looking at me like that before I do something about it."

She wanted him to. She really did. But there were things to settle first, so she dropped her gaze with a shy smile. "Okay," she said. "I'll freshen up."

While she fixed her makeup and added a touch of perfume, he stared down at the computer on her desk. A piece of new software was lying near it, with a scruffy-looking dog on the cover of the box. He grinned.

"Bought a dog, I see," he drawled as she came back into the living room.

She saw where he was looking and laughed self-consciously. "It sounded cute. And it is."

"Told you so. Ready to go?"

She nodded, grabbing her purse.

He stopped her just at the door before he opened it. "Does that lipstick come off easily?" he asked in a deep, lazy tone.

She was barely breathing. "It isn't supposed to."

"Let's see."

He drew her to him, stared into her eyes until she felt her whole body vibrate with delicious sensations, and only then bent to take her mouth completely under his.

Absence had certainly made the heart grow

fonder, she thought while she could. The purse dropped to the floor for the second time that afternoon, and her arms stretched up to hold him while the warm, hard kiss went on and on.

She was standing on her tiptoes when he stopped. His blue eyes, more vivid than she remembered them, stared straight into her green ones with all the evasions and teasing gone.

He was so somber that the expression on his face made her nervous.

"Tell me the job means more to you than I do," he said roughly. "And I'll leave right now before this goes any further."

Her eyelids flinched at the very thought. She drew in an unsteady breath. "It's been weeks," she managed to say in a tight tone.

"Hell, it's been years," he muttered, and his mouth came down on hers again. But this time it was rough, hard, insistent. This time it burrowed into hers with passion and purpose, and she was shaking when he lifted his head.

She held on for dear life. "If you go, I'm going with you," she said involuntarily, her face flushed, her eyes sparkling with feeling.

"That's what I came all this way to hear,"

he said in a harsh undertone. "It took you long enough!"

She burrowed against him and his arms came around to enfold her. "I'm still afraid, Luke," she whispered.

"Everyone's afraid. Not only of falling in love, but of getting married, having children. These are big steps, important steps. People who aren't afraid to take them are the ones who end up divorced and miserable. You have to be sure, but even then, it's a risk."

"I'm willing to take it, if you are," she said after a minute.

His arms contracted again as he bent over her head and rocked her against him. "I've been willing to take it since the first time I saw you," he breathed. "I've spent my life waiting for a woman I could live with. And you didn't even like me!"

She laughed with delight. "Only at first," she protested.

"Ha!" he murmured. "You fought me every step of the way." He lifted his head to look down at her. "Jacobsville can always use a good public defender," he said firmly. "There are kids in trouble everywhere."

She smiled ruefully. "I was hedging," she confessed. "I couldn't bear the thought of being near you all the time if...well, if I was the only one who felt this way."

"Which way?" he asked in a soft, sensuous tone.

She stared at his tie. It was blue and had a paisley pattern—very nice. His thumbs jabbed her gently in the ribs.

"Which way?" he persisted.

She leaned her forehead against him. "I love you."

There was a long, ominous silence. She lifted her head apprehensively and saw his eyes. They were such a vivid blue that they almost glowed. She got barely a glimpse of them before they closed as he lifted her against him and kissed her again. Under his breath, she heard him repeat the words back to her. And then, she stopped trying to hear anything except the beat of her own heart.

Long, tempestuous minutes later, he looked down at her, where she lay in the crook of his arm on the sofa, her body soft and fluid against his, her dress unfastened, her hair disheveled.

His shirt was open, too, the tie long gone, and her fingers played lazily through the wedge of blond hair on his chest.

"We were going out to eat," she reminded him.

"To hell with food. I'm not hungry."

"Well, I am," she said, laughing. "Especially now."

He traced a slow pattern on the lace of her bra. "Spoilsport," he murmured. "Just when I'm getting to know all about you."

She laughed again, moving his hand aside so that she could button up her dress again. "You stop that," she teased.

"Stop? I haven't even gotten started!" he protested.

"There's plenty of time for all that," she reminded him. She searched his blue eyes. "I want a white wedding. Do you mind?"

"I want a white wedding, too," he agreed, smiling at her. "We'll have the works, a best man, a best woman, a flower girl—my niece, of course," he added with a chuckle.

"I'll have my sister-in-law for matron of honor. Best woman," she scoffed, and broke up laughing at the thought of pretty Marianne in a suit and bow tie.

"It will be an occasion," he said. "And then we'll raise cattle and look after kids and grow old together."

She snuggled close to him, so happy that she could barely contain it all. "I love the way that sounds."

"So do I. But we'll grow old slowly, if you don't mind. I've got a lot of ginger left in me, yet."

"I noticed," she said demurely.

He loomed over her with intent. "Did you, now?" he murmured, his eyes drawing over her sensually.

"I love you," she whispered.

He smiled slowly. "I love you, too."

It was the last thing they said for a long time.

The wedding was truly a Jacobsville occasion. Everybody came, even glowering Cy Parks, who wore a suit and brought a wedding present. Ward Jessup and a very pregnant Marianne were present, along with Marianne's Aunt Lillian. Elysia Craig Walker and her husband, Tom, welcomed Belinda into the family, and their daughter Crissy acted as flower girl. Belinda was exquisite in a white lace gown with a train and a delicate lace veil. She carried a bouquet of white rosebuds and she wept when her devastatingly handsome new husband lifted the veil and saw her for the first time as his wife.

Outside the church, the Craig ranch's cowboys made a double line and threw confetti as the happy couple erupted from the front entrance. One of the cowboys had just graduated from high school and was the newest employee on the place. He wore a ten-gallon hat, a red bandanna, boots, jeans, a chambray shirt and a huge toothy smile—and his name was Edward Kells.

The happy couple waved at him as they rushed past to the limousine that would take them to the ranch to change clothes before they went on to the reception Matt Caldwell was hosting for them at his elegant mansion on the outskirts of Jacobsville.

They piled into the car and the driver pulled away from the curb.

Luke looked at Belinda with his whole heart

in his eyes. ''The best day of my life,'' he murmured, ''Mrs. Craig.''

''And the best day of mine, Mr. Craig,'' she echoed.

The words exemplified their vow of love. He drew her close and kissed her. Behind them, the crowd drew in on itself to rehash the details of the elegant society wedding. But inside the limousine, two pairs of sparkling eyes were already looking ahead to a bright and beautiful future.

CHRISTOPHER

"But there's nothing half so sweet in life
As love's young dream."

—Thomas Moore
Love's Young Dream, st. I

Chapter 1

Tansy Deverell was missing again. In fact, she'd been missing for a week. It disturbed Christopher Deverell when he couldn't find his mother, who was in her seventies. More particularly, it disturbed him when the famous Lassiter Detective Agency of Houston, Texas, couldn't find her. Chris had come home from a trip to Spain to find the family in an uproar over the matriarch's disappearance. Tansy was known for her madcap life-style, and she tended to cause scandals wherever she went.

Chris's older brother Logan lived in Houston with his wife, Kit, and their new son, Bryce. Since Logan's marriage, Tansy had become even wilder than usual. She was a diabetic who was on insulin and had to watch her diet very carefully, and Chris worried that she might indulge too much in her travels. Her last escapade had almost landed her in a harem in the Middle East. For a woman in her early seventies, Tandy was adventurous indeed. Old age, she often said, would have to run very fast in order to catch up with her. She wasn't kidding.

On a whim, Chris had traveled to Jacobsville, Texas, to see his cousin Emmett Deverell. In the past, nobody visited Emmett unless they were nuts, but now that Emmett had married Melody and they'd settled down nicely with his three children from his first marriage, Emmett had mellowed. He managed a ranch for Ted Regan, in which he now had a partnership. Things were looking prosperous there, and Tansy might have detoured to visit them. But she hadn't. Chris met with disappointment. Emmett hadn't seen nor heard from Tansy in months.

Chris drove into town and had lunch at the

local high-class restaurant, sitting alone at a corner table with his steak and salad while he brooded about his mother. Logan hadn't been overly concerned. It was amusing how the brothers had changed over the years. In the past, Logan was the straitlaced, worrying one. Now, he was more relaxed and less anxious, especially since his marriage. On the other hand, Chris had been almost as madcap as their mother when he was younger, and women had passed through his life like butterflies. He was thirty-three, and a devastating automobile accident had left him with a different view of the world. His once-handsome face was now less pleasing to the eye, two long furrows having been carved into one lean cheek by shattered glass. He'd lost the sight in one eye, although plastic surgery had spared him deformity. But nothing seemed to erase the scars completely, and he was too weary of hospitals and skin grafts to pursue them further.

He wasn't repulsive by any stretch of the imagination. His smooth olive complexion was enhanced by liquid black eyes with thick black lashes and eyebrows, and a chiseled mouth that was more sardonic than amused most of the time. He had a lean face and a tall, lean, muscular body that was more attractive than ever since his weeks of sailing near the coast of Spain with an old friend. He enjoyed the challenge of the sea, where he could pit his muscle against the waves and wind. A man with as much money as he'd inherited from his father could do whatever pleased him. Unlike Logan, who enjoyed working at the family investment firm, Chris had invested his inheritance in multinational corporations and tripled it in less than ten years. He could live comfortably off the interest, and he'd never found an adequate reason to work a routine job. He dabbled in designing yachts with the friend with whom he'd been sailing in Spain. His ideas were innovative, and one of his designs had taken its owner into the finals of the America's Cup race. He was paid for that idea, and for several others that had sold well.

He watched his investments like a hawk. But increasing his means no longer satisfied him. The carefree bachelor's existence that was such fun in his early twenties was distasteful to him now. He no longer sized up women as potential conquests or enjoyed the attention of pretty fortune-hunters. He felt jaded and life was suddenly empty.

He fingered his coffee cup absently, the motion bringing the waitress with a refill.

"Can I get you anything else?" she asked pleasantly, sizing up his expensive suit and shoes with practiced expertise.

He shook his head. "Thanks. I'm fine."

He didn't encourage her to stay and chat. She was young and pretty, but so were dozens of other women. He envied Logan his family life. Maybe marriage wasn't so bad a thing. Certainly that baby was a delightful little bundle. Chris had never been around children much, but he adored his new nephew and spent a lot of time shopping for educational toys to bring him. That had amused Tansy, who'd suggested that Chris get married and have children of his own.

He'd only shrugged it off with a smile. He'd never had a serious relationship with a woman. His romantic encounters over the years had been light and pleasant and brief. Now he felt as if he'd missed something. Except for his friend who built yachts, he had no one who was close to him. Most of his old girlfriends were married. He traveled alone, ate alone, slept alone. He felt ancient, especially since the wreck.

"Excuse me, but aren't you Christopher Deverell?"

The voice was quiet, unhurried, with a pleasant huskiness. He turned his head to find the face that went with it. Not bad, he thought. Pale gray eyes, pretty complexion, rounded chin, bow mouth, short blond hair with a wave over the pencil-thin eyebrow.

She looked like something out of the thirties, he mused.

"How would you know who I am?" he asked indifferently.

"It's my job." She produced a pad and pen. "I work for the Weatherby News Service. We're not as big as the Associated Press, but we're working hard to catch up," she added with a faint smile. The smile faded quickly. "We're trying to locate your mother, as it happens."

He lifted his hot coffee to his mouth. "Join the club."

"She's gone into hiding," she continued.

"Not that I blame her, under the circumstances, but..."

"Sit down," he said curtly. "You're on my blind side."

"Your...what?"

He turned his head and looked fully at her, so that she could see the extent of the damage the accident had done to his once-handsome face. The black eye in the socket above the two deep scars and just below a smaller one stared straight ahead, but without sight. The nerve damage had been extensive.

She caught her breath audibly and sat down, visibly flustered. "I'm sorry!" she said. "I didn't realize..."

"Most people don't, until they look at me for a while," he added with a mocking smile. He leaned back in the chair, pulling his jacket away from the thin white shirt that covered his broad, hair-roughened chest. In the position, the muscles were visible, and the woman quickly averted her eyes, as if looking at him that way embarrassed her.

"About your mother," she continued.

"First things first. Who are you?"

She hesitated. "I'm Della Larson."

He nodded. "Do you have some idea where my mother might be?"

"Of course." She turned back a few pages in the small flip notebook. "When last seen, she was in a little town just outside London, called Back Wallop." She glanced at him. "That's a village."

"And what would she be doing there?"

"That's where *he* lives," she replied, surprised.

"He, who?" he asked with a broad scowl.

"Look here, she's your mother," she returned. "Don't you know that she was involved with an MP?"

"A Member of Parliament?" he exclaimed.

"Oh, yes, Lord Cecil Harvey. He belonged to the House of Lords and was a relative of the Windsors." She shook her head. "I can't believe you don't know this!"

"I've been on holiday in Spain," he said.

"It's been all over the tabloids," she continued.

His face hardened. "I don't read the scandal sheets," he said tersely.

"Considering how many times you're featured in them, I guess not," she agreed pleasantly. "You had the front page of most of them for two weeks when that Italian countess accused you of fathering her child—"

"We were discussing my mother," he interrupted curtly.

She grimaced. "Sorry. I guess that hit a nerve. Anyway, Mrs. Deverell was photographed coming out of a London hotel with Lord Harvey. There were rumors that he was going to divorce his wife and marry her."

He put the coffee cup down audibly. "My mother?"

"Your mother." She studied him curiously. "You don't look at all like her," she commented. "She has blue eyes and a very fair complexion, almost girlishly pretty."

"My brother and I take after our father. He was Spanish."

"Spanish?" She frowned and flipped quickly through the notebook. "That's not what I was told. They said your father was French, a member of the nobility."

"Our stepfather was French," he returned, and refused to even think of the man, despite the many years it had been since he'd seen him. "Our father died when I was pretty young. Tansy remarried. Several times," he added drolly and picked up his coffee cup again.

"Oh, I see." She was watching him closely. "Why isn't your father mentioned?"

He chuckled. "He was a minor businessman until he bought a few cheap shares of stock and put them away in a safe-deposit box. Long after his death, the box was discovered and opened, and Logan and I inherited a small fortune."

"What was the stock?" she asked suspiciously.

He lifted the coffee cup to his chiseled mouth. "Standard Oil."

She grinned at him. "Amazing foresight."

He shook his head. "Sheer damned luck. He didn't know beans about investments."

"They say your brother does. And so do you."

He chuckled. "I dabble. Not much." His dark eyes narrowed. "Why are you trying to track down Tansy?"

"Why do you call her Tansy instead of 'Mother'?"

"She isn't old enough emotionally to be

anyone's mother," he said simply. "Logan and I grew up trying to keep her out of trouble, with occasional and brief assistance from her five husbands."

"Five?" She glanced at her notes. "I only found four."

"You haven't answered my question."

She fingered the notebook and stared at it instead of him. "I blew a story, a really big one. I'm going to get fired unless I can make amends somehow. I can't lose my job. I have...responsibilities." She lifted her pale eyes to his. "I want to find your mother before the rest of the media can. I want an exclusive interview."

"Ask her for one."

"I can't find her. She's left Back Wallop and nobody knows where she went."

He finished his coffee. "Don't look at me. I can't find her, either, not even with the help of the best detective agency in the state."

She gnawed her lower lip worriedly. "I guess it's understandable that she wouldn't want to be found."

"Thank you for noticing," he said in a tone that dripped sarcasm. "A woman being accused of breaking up a marriage wouldn't rush to find the media.''

Her eyebrows went up. They were pencil thin, very dark despite her blond hair, and quite interesting. ''That's not why she's running, of course.''

''It isn't?''

She sighed heavily. ''Mr. Deverell, I already know the truth. There's no sense in pretending you don't know what's going on.''

''I'm not pretending.''

''Have it your own way.'' She put the pad into her large purse and stood up, slinging it over her shoulder.

''Giving up so soon?'' he taunted.

''I've got to get to England before somebody beats me to the story. It will make my career if I can get it before the others do.''

He stared at her with something like contempt. ''By all means, ruin a life. You and your colleagues put a high price on your own careers, don't you? Nobody else's pain or suffering is too much to ask.''

She flushed. ''You make us sound perverted.''

"I don't, actually." His eyes darkened. "You are perverted. All of you."

She stiffened. "We don't make the news."

"No, you just spread it around, with as many embellishments and enhancements as your editors see fit." He got to his feet, too, and looked down at her. She barely came to his chin. She noticed the discrepancy in their heights and stepped back a few inches.

"Frightened?" he chided, his black eyes glittering as he smiled down at her. "I'm not much of a threat these days."

"You'd be a threat if you were missing both legs," she muttered uncomfortably. The proximity was making her legs wobble. She backed up again. "I'm not responsible for what a few renegade reporters do."

"I know several families, including one royal one, who could give a chilling response to that remark."

Her fingers clutched the strap of her shoulder bag tightly. He noticed her nails, short and rounded and unpolished. The suit she was wearing was of the chain-store variety, and not new. Her shoes were scuffed, vinyl instead of leather, like her purse. He stared at her with

new interest. She wasn't a successful professional, judging by her looks.

"As unfair as it seems, we are judged by the
company we keep," he said quietly. "Some of
your colleagues have no scruples and no conscience."

"I'm not like that."

"Yes, you are," he said simply. "Otherwise, why would you be chasing my mother
over an indiscretion?"

"That's a rather weak thing to call it," she
pointed out.

"What, a would-be affair?"

Her lips parted. "Mr. Deverell, Lord Harvey's body was found just this morning floating naked in the Thames. Your mother is Scotland Yard's number one suspect."

He caught his breath. The shock and terror
he felt were in his stiff expression, his
clenched jaw.

"You really didn't know, did you?" she
asked worriedly. "I'm most dreadfully sorry.
I thought…"

He caught her by the upper arm long enough
to look at his check and lay a five-dollar bill

down with it before he propelled her out the door.

"A cup of coffee doesn't cost five dollars," she murmured as he took her out through the doorway.

"I know how little waiters and waitresses get paid. What business is it of yours?" he asked curtly.

"Could you let me go?"

"Not on your life. You're not making my mother front page news. I've got you and I'm keeping you until I get to the bottom of this."

"You can't! It's kidnapping. It's against the law!"

"Big deal," he muttered. "Come on."

He put her into his big Lincoln on the driver's side and got right in beside her, quickly pressing the master lock switch on his door so that she couldn't open hers. She fumed and pushed, but she was trapped.

"Put on your seat belt," he said.

She did, only because when he put the car into gear and took off, she didn't want to go into the back seat the hard way.

"You drive like a maniac!" she exclaimed.

"So I've been told."

"Listen here, I'm not going anywhere with you. Let me out!"

"When we get to the airport," he assured her.

Her eyebrows lifted. "The airport?"

"We're going to London. You're resourceful and you have contacts that I lack." He glanced at her formidably. "You're going to help me find Tansy."

"Oh, am I, now?" she returned haughtily. "And what am I going to get out of it?"

"A front page scoop when we clear her name."

"You're nuts!"

He nodded. "Apparently."

"But I can't leave the country. Not like this. I told you, I have responsibilities."

"So have I. They'll wait until you get back."

"But I must stay," she persisted.

He lifted the cell phone from its cradle in the floorboard and handed it to her. "Call somebody and make arrangements."

She hesitated, but only for a minute. She couldn't afford to miss the opportunity of a lifetime, which this certainly was. Once she got the story, she'd file it no matter what he tried to do. If she didn't go with him, he might find some way to block her, to keep her from finding his mother. That wouldn't do at all.

She punched in the number and then the button that would send the call along the airways. It rang once, twice, three times.

"Hello?"

She smiled at the pepper in that sweet old voice. "Hi. It's me. I just wanted to tell you that I'm going to be out of town for a day or two. You let Mrs. Harris come over and cook for you. I'll make it right when I get home."

"Chasing after that mad old lady, are you?" A deep chuckle came from the other end of the line. "Just like me, when I was younger."

"Not just like you," she replied, smiling. "You used to hang out in bars with the Lafayette Escadrille and the SAS. I just walk in your shadow."

"Flatterer!"

"Don't forget to put the chain latch on at night," she added worriedly. "And if you need me..."

Chris already had the picture, from the brief snatches of conversation he overheard. "Give

him this number,'' he told her without taking
his eyes from the road—a good thing, at the
speed they were going. He recited the cell
phone number, and then added one with a foreign exchange. ''That's in London. He can call
anytime if he needs you. I'll make sure the call
is forwarded immediately.''

She relayed the information.

''Sounds young,'' the old man cackled. ''Is
he?''

''Sort of,'' she replied warily. ''Stay warm,
too. Don't worry about turning up the heat.
Okay?''

''Okay. Now stop worrying about me and
get the job done. Don't shame us.''

''I wouldn't dare!'' she chuckled. ''I'll see
you when I get back, Grandad.''

''You take care, too. You're the only family
I got left.''

''Same here.'' She smiled as she put the receiver down. She glanced at the taciturn man
beside her warily. ''Thanks.''

He shrugged. ''You'll do better sleuthing if
you're not worried. Your grandfather sounds
like a character.''

''He was, and still is. He was a reporter during the gang wars in Chicago, during Prohibition, and after that he was a war correspondent." She laughed. "He can tell some stories. I followed in his footsteps, but not very well. I'm not sure I'm cut out for investigative reporting after all."

"What did you do before?"

"I did political news and features." She grimaced. "I was good at it, too, but Grandad said I was wilting on the vine and wasting away. He wanted me to do something exciting and risky while I was still young enough."

"Don't you have any other family?"

She shook her head. "My parents died overseas. They were touring the Middle East when the plane they were in was shot down accidentally. Grandad took me in when I was just ten and raised me."

"Tough luck," he said. "No brothers, sisters, uncles or aunts?"

"An aunt," she replied. "She lives in California and never writes." She glanced at him. "At least you have a brother."

"A brother and a mother," he replied.

"What's she like?"

"She's a hell-raiser," he returned amusedly.

"I've never known her when she wasn't in trouble. But she doesn't kill people," he added firmly.

"I hope you're right," she replied.

"I know I am." But there was the faintest doubt in his voice. He turned the car onto the highway that led to the Jacobsville airport, new lines in his worried face.

Chapter 2

Heathrow Airport was busy, especially for the time of year. Summer was high season for most tourists, and as Chris passed along the crowded path to the customs line, he heard accents from countries all over the world. He glanced at Della, surprised by the look on her face. She seemed overly affected by her surroundings, by the people around her. Some were wearing exotic dress, and she seemed to find those fascinating.

He had a sudden thought. "You have your passport, but you've never been out of the States before, have you?" he asked.

She glanced at him with a shy smile. "Actually, I haven't. I always wanted to travel like my grandfather did, so I applied for my passport, but I couldn't afford to go anywhere until I landed this latest job. Now that I can, I've been too afraid to leave him on his own. He's diabetic, you see, and he won't leave sweets alone. He's been in a coma twice in the past three years, because he's too stubborn to admit there's anything wrong with him."

"That sounds familiar," Chris murmured under his breath. He glanced at the line beside them, which had thinned considerably. He took Della's arm and steered her and her wheeled suitcase to the shorter line.

"You know how to do this, don't you?" she asked, impressed.

"I spend a lot of time overseas," he commented. "Got your ticket?"

"Right here." She held it up.

They passed through customs and baggage control with a minimum of fuss, and Chris went right to the rental car agency to hire a vehicle. Minutes later, they were on the way to their hotel, to check in. He seemed to find driving on the left-hand side of the road very easy. It made Della nervous, but after the first few minutes, she relaxed and began to pay attention to the sights.

"We'll leave the luggage, get a bite to eat, and head out for Back Wallop," he said.

"I'm glad to see you aren't planning to let jet lag hold you back," she commented dryly.

He lifted an eyebrow and smiled. "What do you know about jet lag?"

"I've read lots of travel books. Besides, my grandfather is an authority. As I mentioned before, he was a war correspondent."

"In which war?"

"World War II, Korea, Vietnam, and several other little wars in Hispanic countries."

"I'm impressed."

"He can tell some stories," she mused. "It's killing him that he can't do it anymore. He's seventy-three, and he's got arthritis as well as diabetes. It's like he's given up on life because he's been slowed down."

"Tansy has the same problem," he confided. "She thinks like a sixteen-year-old, but her body can't do what her mind wants it to."

"She must be a fascinating person."

"I've always thought so," he said. "My

earliest memories of my mother are flamboy-
ant, colorful images. She was always going
somewhere, hosting parties, dragging us to
cultural events like opera and the theater.'' He
shook his head. ''She used to be just a little
less reckless.'' His face sobered. ''I can't believe she'd get herself mixed up in a murder.
It's not like her.''

''Anyone can get in a circumstance where
violence becomes the only answer,'' she said,
glancing out the window at the crowded
streets. ''Are we downtown?''

''Yes. And here's our hotel.'' He pulled off
the road into an elegant courtyard, where a
man dressed like something out of medieval
times was opening and closing car doors for
guests.

''It's very elegant,'' she commented.

''When I travel, I always go first-class,'' he
said carelessly. ''I find it's less wearing to be
pampered, especially if you've been to more
than one or two countries on business.''

''I thought you didn't work,'' she said.

He gave her an incredulous glance. ''I inherited money, but I have to work at keeping
it,'' he said. ''I own interests in businesses all

over the world, in several multinational corporations. I like to know where my money's going, and how it's being spent.''

''So that's how it's done,'' she murmured.

He chuckled. ''Stick with me, kid. I'll make an entrepreneur of you in no time.''

''That would be nice,'' she said. ''I think I'd like making a fortune.'' She shrugged. ''Well, I'd like the challenge of making it,'' she added thoughtfully. ''Money's not really very important to me, except that I'd like to spoil Grandad a little while I've still got him. He sacrificed a lot to bring me up.''

The uniformed man opened the door for Della and helped her out, while he signaled for a porter to take the luggage from the boot, which Christopher had already opened automatically from the driver's side.

Chris escorted Della to the front desk and registered them, in separate double rooms. He handed her the encoded card key and led the way into the elevator.

''You look embarrassed,'' he commented.

She was. The clerk had asked if they were sharing a room. She felt uncomfortable. ''Sorry,'' she murmured. ''I'm not used to sophisticated circles. I guess they get a lot of unmarried couples here and nobody thinks anything about it. I'm a little out of step with the rest of the world.''

He was gaping at her. She was an anachronism, all right. It probably came from being raised by a man from a different generation.

"No love life?" he teased.

She didn't rise to the bait. "Not now," she replied.

He paused while they got off on the fifth floor. He showed her how to work the card key.

"The bellhop will bring the luggage up shortly," he promised. "Meanwhile, I'll freshen up and drop by to pick you up on the way out of the hotel." He hesitated. "Ever eaten fish and chips?"

"Not real English ones," she said.

He grinned. "You've got a treat in store."

They stopped at a roadside stand and gobbled down fish and chips and strong tea to the foreign sound of proper English being spoken all around them. Della was delighted with the new experience.

"Later, we'll have a proper, sit-down meal," he promised. "But there isn't time now. I want to find Tansy."

"Oh, this is lovely," she protested. "I'm enjoying it!"

He chuckled. "So I see."

She was standing on his right side, so that he could see her and vice versa. He looked very worried, and she wondered how she'd feel if it was her grandfather the police and the press were chasing.

She put down her cup of tea, frowning.

"What's wrong?" he asked.

"I was thinking how I'd feel, in your place," she said, looking up at him with darkened gray eyes. "Grandad is my whole life."

He searched her face and nodded slowly. "Tansy and Logan are the only close family I have. I didn't worry so much about them several years ago. Since I've had the wreck, my perspective has changed." He looked grim.

"Life is short, and you hadn't realized how short before," she speculated.

His eyebrows jerked. "That's it, exactly. I had a concussion, internal and external injuries, as well as the damage to my left eye. It took months for me to get back on my feet, and I'll never regain the sight in my eye. It woke me up.''

''I remember reading about you in the tabloids, when you were younger,'' she recalled. ''You were like your mother, forever in and out of scrapes and scandals.''

''Not anymore,'' he said. ''It isn't worth the risk.''

''What is?'' she asked solemnly.

He turned and looked down at her pensively. ''Leaving the world a little better than we found it,'' he said simply.

She smiled. ''I like that.''

He touched his finger to the tip of her small nose and smiled. ''I like you,'' he said genuinely, and chuckled when she flushed prettily.

''Are you sure? I thought I was at the top of your enemies list.''

He shook his head. ''You don't fit the image of a hardened newshound,'' he said simply. He frowned slightly. ''In fact, I don't think you have what it takes to do the job properly. You've got too much heart. Eventually, you'll be wrung out like a damp cloth.''

She stiffened. ''I've been a reporter for sev-

eral years and I can do this job,'' she asserted
stubbornly. "Grandad says I just have to put
aside my hang-ups and concentrate on the process of gathering information."

"Your grandad can probably eat lunch while
he watches war footage," he replied. "I expect
he's grown such a hard shell over the years
that nothing much affects him."

He was right. She hated admitting it. "He
said he was sensitive when he started out,
too."

"Bull. He'd have gotten over that the first
day in the field." His eyes narrowed. "Can
you really see yourself printing everything you
find out about peoples' intimate lives behind
the social masks they wear? Can you destroy
a marriage by turning in stories on unfaithful
spouses or headline-making news about their
private sexual perversions? That sort of news
destroys lives, Della. Are you really hard
enough to hurt people deliberately for the sake
of making headlines?"

He was asking the same questions she'd
asked herself. He made her uncertain, unsure
of herself. He made her ashamed. She didn't

answer him. Instead, she wiped her mouth on the napkin and put it on her plate.

He glanced at his watch. "Are you finished? We need to get started."

"Yes. I'm through." She finished her last swallow of tea and didn't look at him as she got up from the counter and left him to pay the bill. She started down the road toward the thick of the commercial district, thinking how ancient this country was and how many empires had embraced it. The history of Great Britain had always fascinated her, and now here she was in London itself, and she was too sick at heart to pay much attention to sights she'd always dreamed of seeing.

She felt Chris's hard fingers close around her elbow as he escorted her back to the car and put her in what would be, in the United States, the driver's side of the car. The steering wheel was on the right side, here.

"Curious feeling, isn't it?" he asked with a smile.

"Very."

He got in and cranked the engine. "Tell me everything you know about the murder," he asked.

"Well, honestly, I don't know a lot," she had to confess. "I was told that the late member of parliament was found floating in the river with a blunt-force injury to the right temple. The official cause of death was drowning, though."

"The right temple? You're sure?"

"I'm sure."

He looked a little relieved, oddly, but he pulled out into traffic again and the moment for questions passed.

Della was enchanted with the English countryside. She was full of questions, to which Chris seemed to know most of the answers. She was surprised to find him something of an authority on Tudor history.

"I'll bet you watch every British drama special on Henry VIII that comes on television," she said with a chuckle.

"I do. And pick holes in most of them," he added. "History isn't exciting enough for visual displays, because it happens over such a long period of time. In order for it to be palatable for the masses, it has to be compressed, and that distorts it. But I take fiction for what it is, simply entertainment, and I enjoy it just the same."

"I like Native American history," she said. "The Indians got a raw deal."

"Everybody got a raw deal," he countered. "What about the Irish who starved by the thousands during the great potato famine and received no outside help? How about the political prisoners who died in concentration camps in Nazi Germany, or the Russian people that Stalin purged? In fact, what about the French Huguenots who had to flee Europe or be slaughtered?"

"Good grief," she exclaimed.

"That's not a fraction of the whole," he continued. "Civilizations long gone had their own vicious persecutions and slavery. Our own ancestors were probably among that number. Otherwise why would they have come to America in the first place? They were looking for something they didn't have in their own countries."

She smiled at him. "You're very interesting to talk to," she said unexpectedly.

He burst out laughing. "That's new," he murmured. He didn't glance toward her; she was on his blind side, and it would have been dangerous to turn his head far enough to see her face. But she was already becoming a vivid portrait deep in his mind.

"I don't understand."

He gave a turn signal and pulled out onto a long highway. "In my younger days, I was what most people refer to as a rake," he commented. "And I only dated a certain type of woman, very sophisticated and modern, if you get my meaning."

She did. She cleared her throat. "I see."

He smiled reflectively. "How I've changed," he murmured.

The wry comment caught her attention. "Why have you changed?"

"Perhaps I'm not as confident as I was," he said thoughtfully. "The scars depress me sometimes, when I look in a mirror. They could probably get rid of the rest of them, but I am so tired of hospitals and doctors."

She studied him covertly for a moment before she shifted her eyes back to the road ahead of them. "The scars look rakish, you know," she murmured.

"Do they?"

He didn't sound amused. "I know it must have been terribly painful," she added quickly.

"I'm not offended. I've gotten used to it, I guess. But I miss having the sight in both eyes."

"Of course you do. I only meant that you aren't disfigured."

"So I've been told." He stopped at a sign-post that indicated the way to Back Wallop. "Well, something's gone right today," he said, indicating the sign. "From the map, I'd say we're about ten minutes away. I hope we can trace her," he added uneasily. "England's a big country."

"You've always found her before, haven't you?"

"Yes. But we had private detectives on the case," he corrected. "And I don't dare involve them again now, under the circumstances. Dane Lassiter, who does investigative work for our family, was a Texas Ranger. Regardless of his sympathies, he'd follow the law all the way and make no apologies for doing it."

"In other words, he'd turn your mother in," she decided. "Is he really that hard-nosed?"

"Less so since he married and had a family, but he's still a law-and-order man. I didn't want to put him on the spot." He smiled grimly. "I wish I'd paid more attention to those lectures on criminal justice in college."

"Did you graduate?" she asked.

He shook his head. "I was too busy drinking and carousing to pay much attention in class. I dropped out in my sophomore year. It's no great loss," he assured her. "I inherited more than most college graduates make in a lifetime."

"So you just have fun."

He shrugged. "Up until the wreck, I didn't know another way to live." He turned fully toward her, so that he could see her face. "Things are more complicated now. I'm rather sorry that I wasted so much of my life on trivial things." He searched her soft eyes and smiled warmly. "You're a pretty little thing," he murmured, liking the way she flushed. "I'd have had you for breakfast a few years ago. But you'd lie on my conscience like lead."

"You'd be lucky," she murmured coolly. "I don't think much of casual affairs or people who have them."

"I noticed."

She shifted uncomfortably. "Shouldn't we be going?"

"We should."

He turned the car toward Back Wallop. He was glad he'd insisted that Della come along on this trip, although he wasn't quite sure why. She appealed to him as none of his casual conquests ever had; probably because she was a unique commodity in his carefree life. Logan would say he was losing his grip on reality, but Chris thought he was only just finding a handhold. He realized as he drove down the narrow road that he'd never really thought ahead very far. Della made him think about houses in the country and flower gardens. He scowled, because they were unfamiliar feelings. He'd never felt them with other women. Not that his sort of woman would waste her time planting flowers, he mused. He wondered how Della would look in a blue silk gown, sprawled on black silk sheets...

The direction of his thoughts brought him crashing back to the present. He couldn't afford that sort of lapse, not with this woman.

She was the wedding ring sort. He'd better remember it, too.

They arrived in the small village of Back Wallop fifteen minutes later and parked beside a news agent's shop.

"Best place to ask questions, if we aren't too obvious," he pointed out, as he opened the door for her and helped her out of the small car.

"With our accents, we'll blend right in," she said, tongue-in-cheek.

He chuckled softly. "Never mind that. Just follow my lead." He curled her fingers into his, tightening his grip when she pulled back, and walked her into the store.

"Mornin'," the proprietor greeted them with a speculative glance. "Need help, guv?"

"Just directions, thanks," Chris said with a warm smile. "The wife and I are over here to visit my cousins, the Duke of Marlboro and his wife, Lady Gail, but we just heard about Lord Harvey and thought we'd swing through Back Wallop on the way and pay our respects to Lady Harvey. Could you direct us?"

"Your cousin is the Duke of Marlboro, you say?" The man was impressed.

"Yes. Do you know Georgie?"

He cleared his throat. No, he didn't, and even if he had he wouldn't presume to call his lordship the duke "Georgie."

"Lady Harvey lives just down the road in Carstairs Manor. It's to the left just across the bridge as you round the curve. Can't miss it. Sad about the old man."

"Yes, it is. Thank you," Chris said. "Ready to go, darling?" he added, pulling Della close to his side and looking down at her with an expression on his face that made her knees wobble. She colored again and nodded, not trusting her voice.

"Newlyweds, aren't yer?" the shopkeeper said with a grin. "Anyone could see it. You're in luck, there, guv, she's a beauty."

"Don't I know it?" Chris murmured, with a wink in her direction. "Let's get going, old girl. Thanks for the help," he added over his shoulder.

"Sure thing." The shopkeeper chuckled to himself, watching them go. Chris had put his arm around Della and pulled her close, so that she fit nicely under his arm. They looked good together, the tall dark man and the pretty little blond woman. He sighed, remembering his own youthful marriage. He did miss his wife, he thought, and looking at the couple before him made the ache even deeper. How lucky they were, to have a whole lifetime together to look forward to.

Chris, unaware of the shopkeeper's thoughts, pulled Della even closer as they paused at the passenger side of the automobile.

He tilted her soft round chin up with his fingertips and searched her confused gray eyes. They were soft as summer rain, he thought, oblivious to everything around them. She had a heart the size of the whole world, and she felt so right in his arms. He looked down at her bow of a mouth, pink and pretty and just slightly parted. It would be stupid to do what he was thinking. He realized that, even as his head bent and his mouth fastened gently onto those lovely pink lips. They were every bit as soft as he'd imagined, and they were just faintly unsteady under the gentle pressure. He hesitated, lifting a breath away to see what she wanted. Her fingers were against his thin shirt, barely touching, and then opening, pressing against his chest. The tiny movement was all the encouragement he needed. He bent again, and this time the pressure was neither tender nor brief.

Della felt her heart stop in her chest as his arm contracted and brought her much too close to his tall, fit body. His mouth was warm and hard and devastatingly expert. He did things to her lips that she'd never experienced with anyone else, arousing things that made her moan.

The sound brought him out of the trance he'd fallen into. He lifted his head, breathing a little roughly, and looked into her turbulent, shocked eyes.

"You don't know much about kissing for a woman your age," he said, with no expression whatsoever in his lean, handsome face.

She swallowed and tried to steady her breath. "I told you..."

"Kissing won't get you pregnant," he continued relentlessly. "Not even openmouthed kissing. You don't like it at all, do you?"

She felt all too much on the defensive, gauche and untried. She glared up at him from eyes that were still half shocked. "It's a public street!" she said on a nervous laugh.

"Yes, I know, and on a private one, you'd

have fought me," he said flatly. He eased her away, inch by inch. He was scowling, quiet, almost grim. There was a look in her eyes, in her face, that disturbed him.

"Shouldn't we...go?" she asked breathlessly.

"Probably," he agreed. He opened the door and seated her before he went around the bonnet and got in beside her. His lean hand hesitated on the switch. "Someone forced you," he commented, staring at her. Her eyelids flinched. "Were you raped?"

She shivered. "Please..."

"Were you raped?"

She lowered her eyes to her lap. "Not... quite."

"Someone you knew?"

"My fiancé," she said dully. "When I broke the engagement two days before the wedding, because I caught him with one of my bridesmaids at the wedding rehearsal supper. He was missing during the toast. I stepped outside to look for him, and I found him, and her, in the back seat of his car." She sighed. It felt good, somehow, to tell someone the truth. She hadn't been able to talk about it with her grandfather. "He took me home. Grandad was out that evening, and when I told Bruce I wouldn't marry him, he was furious and tried to have his way with me. Luckily, he backed down. He said I wouldn't give out, so he found somebody who would, and it was just as well that I was breaking the engagement because he didn't want to spend his life trying to get me aroused."

The pain in her voice softened him. He stared at her quietly. After a minute, his fingers lifted to her short hair and touched it, lightly. "Sometimes people fall into relationships because they're lonely, or frightened. But marriage has to have a physical as well as an emotional foundation. Did you ever want him?"

She shifted nervously. "Not...that way."

"Then it would have been a disaster if you'd married him. Surely you know that now?"

She turned her head and looked at him. She seemed unusually vulnerable. "All that...is wrong," she said. "Isn't it? I mean, after marriage you're supposed to, but outside marriage you..."

His hand stilled. "Don't tell me. You were raised by missionaries."

He was being facetious, but he didn't know how close to the truth he was.

"Yes, my parents were missionaries," she agreed, wide-eyed. "How did you know?"

Chapter 3

Chris smiled ruefully after the surprise wore off. "Well, well," he murmured. "So that's it."

"I guess you've forgotten more about love than I'll ever learn," she mused. She shrugged. "I told you I was a dead bust as a modern woman."

"No, you're not," he argued. "You've got potential," he added in a deep, sensuous tone. "All it needs is developing."

"Are you volunteering?" she asked with a wry smile.

He tugged on a lock of her hair. "Don't tempt me. We've got enough complications without adding that to them. Tansy, remember?"

She grimaced. "Sorry."

"No harm done," he said with a chuckle. He let go of her hair and cranked the car. "First we'll find Tansy and solve her problems. Then we'll have time to devote to our own."

"I don't have a problem."

He gave her a look of mild astonishment. "You don't like French kisses, and you don't think that's a problem?"

She glared at him. "It isn't!"

He smiled slowly. "See what I mean?"

She decided that it would be best if she ignored him, so she tried it for the five minutes it took to get to the manor house.

"This is where things get a little sticky," he said thoughtfully, as they sat at the closed gates where three carloads of reporters were camped out.

"Can't you use the phone over there and tell her we're lost and need directions?" she suggested.

"That wouldn't work. I'll guarantee every one of these newshounds has already tried that angle. I suppose the direct approach is always the best one." He got out of the car, smiled genially at the reporters as he worked his way past them, and picked up the telephone at the gate. He spoke softly so that the reporters couldn't hear him. After a minute he nodded, put the phone down, and got back in the car with Della.

"She's sending a man down for us. I described the car I'm driving," Chris told her.

"What did you say that got her to open the gates?" she asked, astonished.

"I said that I was a relation of the Duke of Marlboro and I needed to speak to her urgently about her late husband."

"And she believed you?"

He chuckled. "As it happens, we know each other," he admitted. "I didn't realize she'd married, which is why I didn't recognize her as Lady Harvey. I knew her as just plain Clothilde Elmore."

Della was immediately jealous and uncomfortable. He didn't say that the woman was an old lover, but she probably was. She hated the thought of those other women, and that was dangerous. She had to remember that she was here on a job, and not to try to catch the eye of this reformed rake—if he was reformed, which she doubted.

"What are you going to tell her when we get to the house?" she persisted.

He stared at her amusedly. "You're the reporter. Hadn't you better start formulating some hard-nosed questions?"

"I guess I had," she agreed, and pulled out her pad.

He covered her hand with his before the other reporters got a look at it. "Not here," he said softly. "They can't know we're infiltrating."

"Oh. Sure." She put the pad up. "I'll just do it mentally."

He looked as if he had doubts about that, but he didn't say another word. In a few minutes, a small car with two passengers shot down the driveway. One man came to Chris's car and climbed in the back. The other man opened the gate. Chris shot through the opening before the reporters could push their way

through. The gate closed to a chorus of jeers
and catcalls from the frustrated onlookers.

"Neat, that," Chris mused as he followed
the other car up the long driveway.

"Damned vultures," the man in the back
seat muttered in a thick Cockney accent.
"Poor Lord Harvey not even buried, and all
this going on. The poor old man. He did so
hate publicity."

"Something I share with the late lord,"
Chris muttered.

The man in the back seat took a good look
at the driver in the rearview mirror. "I know
you," he said suddenly. "You're that Deverell
from America, the one who was caught in bed
with…"

"Never mind," Chris said icily. "That's
past history."

"Well, sure it is, guv, but you must know
how her ladyship feels now," he added.

"Indeed I do," Chris replied.

"She'll be glad of company. Had to live like
a hermit these past two days, what with the
inquisition from the Yard and all." He shook
his head. "Poor old man, poor old lord," he
said sadly, "naked as a jaybird and floating in

the river, all those people taking pictures of him. He was so stately, such a gentleman.... Deverell,'' he repeated suddenly, staring at Chris harder. ''You're her son! It was your mother killed the poor old man!''

''My mother won't kill a fly on her salad,'' Chris said with utter disgust. ''She may be a licensed lunatic, but she's no murderess.''

The man looked vaguely placated. ''You sure of that?''

''I'd stake my life on it. If Lord Harvey was murdered, my mother didn't do it.''

''Had to be murder, don't you see,'' came the heavy reply. ''Had a bruise the size of my fist on the side of his head. He drowned, but he was unconscious when he drowned they say.''

''He was hit on the right side of his head, too, wasn't he?'' Chris asked carelessly.

''Sure was. Right at the temple. The blow was so hard it broke the skull. Sorry, miss,'' he added when he saw Della go white.

Chris glanced at her. ''I told you that you were too soft for the sort of work you do, didn't I?'' he asked bluntly.

"What sort of work does she do, then?" the passenger asked.

"She's trying to make it as a crime novelist," Chris lied with a straight face. "But she gets sick at her stomach when she has to read about real crimes. I think she should write political thrillers, myself."

"That's my sort of book," the passenger said smugly. "Politics is the most interesting thing I know about. Not that most of what you read in the papers is the truth. No, sir."

"I'll agree with that, having been a victim of the gutter press myself," Chris said.

"It's not all gutter press," Della felt compelled to say.

"No, there are some good journalists," Chris agreed. "But then, they don't write for the tabloids!"

Which left Della without a comeback. She stared at the gray stone manor house with real interest. It was the closest she'd ever been to affluence on this scale. The place was surrounded by landscaped lawns and gardens, even a fountain where the driveway circled the house. There was an elegant porch with flower urns everywhere, and a huge garage and tennis court and swimming pool in the back.

"Nice gardens, aren't they?" the passenger said. "The late Lord Harvey was an avid gardener, always puttering out there, he was."

"My mother has the same passion," Chris said, "although she rarely stays home long enough to indulge it. She lived over here some years ago, when I was in boarding school."

"You have English ties, guv?"

"I'm a cousin to the Duke of Marlboro."

"Well, I'll be!"

"And a cousin to the ruling royal family as well," he added on a chuckle. "So you see, Great Britain isn't so foreign to me after all."

"I should say not, sir!"

They pulled up at the front door and the passenger got out quickly to help Della from the small automobile, smiling at her shy thanks.

"I'll put the car around back for you, sir," the passenger said, taking the keys. "Just give us a ring when you're ready to leave. Right-o, then."

A butler answered the door and escorted Della and Chris into the elegant, antique-furnished living room, where the mourning Lady Harvey lay sprawled across the sofa in a gauzy rainbow-colored lounge dress that would have probably financed the entire annual budget of a Third World army.

Chris introduced himself, naming Della as his traveling companion with a finesse that made her blush. Lady Harvey extended her white arm and allowed Chris to kiss her knuckles with a continental air.

"So nice to meet you," the former Clothilde Elmore drawled in a cultured accent. "I'm in mourning, you know, but I look terrible in black. Do sit down."

"I'm sorry about your husband," Chris said.

She waved a hand. "He was in his early seventies, you know, and his health was failing," she said languidly. "Not that I won't miss him, of course, but he was so much older than I."

That was debatable, Della thought. The woman had obviously had several face-lifts, but her throat and hands showed her true age, and she was no spring chicken.

"I'm looking for my mother," Chris continued. "I understand that she's implicated in the homicide."

"*Homicide?* What homicide?" Lady Harvey exclaimed, sitting straight up with a hand to her throat.

"But the tabloids..." Della began.

Lady Harvey burst out laughing, although there was an odd flush in her face. "Good Lord, I had no idea they were spreading such drivel. Harvey was waterskiing in the lake day before yesterday. He came loose, hit his head on the stern of the boat your mother was driving, and drowned. That's all there is to it."

Chris almost fell over with relief. "Thank God!"

"I cannot imagine how anyone could construe this as anything other than a tragic accident," she continued curtly. "What motive would your mother have to murder him anyway? They were old friends through her late husband. The three of them were great pals, although they stopped corresponding when Cecil and I married, of course. I had nothing in common with such hijinks, quite honestly. Your mother was always in the middle of some outrageous circumstance."

"She doesn't know any other way to live," Chris agreed. He scowled. "But if there's no homicide, why is my mother being sought?"

Lady Harvey waved a hand. "I have no idea. The police questioned her, and myself, and went away. My attorney tells me that there is no evidence of foul play and no further investigation is warranted."

"Then I've made a trip for nothing," he said with a smile as he got to his feet. "I'm very grateful to you. But you say you have no idea where my mother might be?"

"None whatsoever, she left the country just after the police came, or so I heard. She didn't tell me where she was going." She thought for a minute. "Bainbridge might know. She and Cecil were friends with him as well. Yes. You might try Lord Bainbridge. He lives just down the road, anyone can direct you."

"Thank you. You've been most gracious, and at such a trying time," Chris said, bending to kiss her hand again.

"Oh, not to worry, I'm grateful for the company. Those dreadful reporters won't go away, God knows why."

"They'll tire eventually and worry someone else," Chris assured her. "Good day."

The car was brought around by the same man who'd accompanied them to the manor house. He waved them off, the gates were opened, and Chris and Della drove through the massed press corps.

"Wait just a minute, please," Della asked as he started to pull out into the main road. She motioned to a woman journalist and rolled the window down.

"She says that there was no murder, and that Scotland Yard has determined that it was an accidental death," she told the brunette. "If that's so, why are you all still out here?"

"She said that?" the journalist asked. "It's news to us. We had word this morning that accidental death has been ruled out and murder charges are pending against a woman named…" She pulled out her pad and read, "Tansy Deverell, an American."

"She said that Lord Harvey was waterskiing, fell and hit his head on the boat's stern and drowned," Della persisted.

"He was knocked unconscious with a blunt object suspected to be a silver cane head," the woman replied. "Mrs. Deverell was known to possess such a cane. The police have it now. And Lord Harvey was found in the river, not in a lake, stark naked."

"I don't understand any of this," Della said heavily.

"Neither do we. But her ladyship up there stands to inherit ten million pounds, and even with inheritance tax, that's a bundle. Furthermore, she's mixed up with some bloke from a militant workers' party—" She stopped dead. "Who are you?"

"I'm an American journalist," Della said honestly. "My paper sent me here to see what I could dig out. Well, you see, Mrs. Deverell *is* an American." She let the implication sink in.

"I see. Wouldn't know something about her, would you?" the woman asked cagily.

"Just that she has claimed to have been kidnapped by aliens once, and a sheikh tried to add her to his harem."

The woman journalist laughed delightedly. "Thanks! She doesn't sound like a murderess, does she? What a delightful old bird! I wish she was my mum."

"So do I," Della said. "Thanks."

"You, too!"

Chris drove off while Della was closing the window. "You didn't have to be so forthcoming!"

"Yes, I did. She gave me information, I gave her information. We're even." She glanced at him, saw the lines of strain. "I still don't think she did it, evidence or no evidence. I'd like to know more about this bloke from the worker's party."

"You looked relieved when they said the MP was hit on the right side of the head. Why?" she asked curiously.

He grinned. "Because Tansy is left-handed. Let's go see Bainbridge. Maybe he can clear some of the details up for us."

Lord Bainbridge could, and did. He was no friend of Lady Harvey, but he knew quite a bit about her.

He brushed back his thick white mustache and leaned his bulk back in his huge armchair by the fireplace. "Tramp, she is, begging your pardon, ma'am," he told Della. "Nothing but a tramp. I warned Cecil about her, but he was so obsessed with her beauty that he wouldn't

rest until he'd married her. Face-lifts and
tummy tucks and war paint and padding, that's
all she was, with a mercenary eye. All of us
could see it. Now she's killed him and she'll
blame poor Tansy to save herself.''

"Tansy isn't a killer," Chris said curtly.

"I know that. We all know that. But she's
the prime suspect. It seems her ladyship has an
ironclad alibi. She was giving a speech at a
children's benefit at the time Cecil died.''

"Nobody can be that precise about the time
of death," Della said flatly. "Especially if his
body was in the water for any length of time.
The water temperature could distort the time
of death by at least two or three hours.''

He shook his head. "He was wearing a
wristwatch and apparently lifted his arm to
ward off the blow. His watch face was cracked
and stopped at what they presume was exactly
the time of death.''

"How convenient," Chris muttered.

"Not convenient. Planned," Della countered. "And devilishly clever.''

"If only Tansy hadn't run," Chris said
heavily. "It's made her look guilty, even if she
isn't.''

"I don't think she ran," Lord Bainbridge confided. "I think she's been taken somewhere for safekeeping so she can't tell her side of the story. I think she saw the murder."

Two pairs of eyes widened. "By whom?"

"By her ladyship's boyfriend," the old man said. "Tony Cartwright. He's a young street tough with a loud mouth and a following. He heads one of the militant groups that wants to oust the ruling party. He's been tossing money around like corn flakes just lately, and he has no visible means of support. My guess is that Lady Harvey has been funding him and her husband found out and made the mistake of confronting her with it. Or maybe he even caught them together in a compromising situation. Cecil was never one to keep his mouth shut. He'd have gone in headfirst."

"And died for it," Chris supposed. His eyes narrowed. "What can we do?"

"My suggestion would be to hire a private detective and have Tony and her ladyship watched," came the immediate reply. "In fact, I have just the man for you. He was with Interpol for a while, and before that, rumor has it, the SAS. He's costly, but he's worth every penny. I can put you in touch, if you like.''

"What's his name?"

Lord Bainbridge smiled. "You can call him Seth."

"Does he have an office?"

Lord Bainbridge shook his head. "He does a lot of hush-hush government work, as a free agent. He takes the occasional private case, if it interests him. Frankly, he doesn't need the money anymore.''

"You think he'll take this case?" Chris asked.

The old man nodded. "I think so. Let me have the name of your hotel and I'll ask him to contact you tonight."

Chris let out a long breath. "You've taken a load off my mind. My mother is a lunatic, but I love her."

"Many of us have, and lost her," the old man said wistfully. "Yes, even me. You have no idea what a beauty she was fifty years ago. I met her in Madrid one summer and never got over her. I'd do anything I could to help her."

"Does Lady Harvey know that?"

He shook his head and chuckled. "Doubt

she'd have sent you to me if she had. She thinks I was best friends with her husband and might feel vengeful. I'm sure she thought I'd slam the door in your face. Tough luck for her," he added grimly.

Della and Chris thanked the old soldier and went back to their London hotel.

Chris was dejected as he left Della at her door. "I'll phone you if Seth gets in touch with me," he said. "Try to get some rest. I don't know where this will lead us, but I hope Lord Bainbridge was wrong about Tansy being held prisoner. This whole damned thing is crazy!"

"Most crimes are, but they make great sense to the perpetrators." She put a soft hand up to his lean cheek. "Try not to worry. It will be all right."

His teeth clenched. He caught her by the upper arms and pulled her to him. "I don't know how I'd have gotten through the day without you," he said huskily, and bent to her mouth.

The words softened her as much as the slow, sweet kiss he pressed on her open lips. She gasped and his own lips opened, pressing deeper. He made a sound under his breath and his hands let go of her arms to catch her hips and pull them deliberately into his.

She pulled away, breathless. "It's...public," she stammered.

He was having trouble getting his own breath. She was delightful, pretty and sweet and intelligent. He'd looked at women as acquisitions until the wreck. Now he saw what he'd been missing for most of his life—a woman with a heart. Perhaps he had to grow old enough to appreciate what was inside instead of outside.

He caught both her hands in his and lifted them to his lips. "You're a treasure," he said quietly. "Thank you for coming to England with me."

"Well, I didn't have a lot of choice, remember," she stammered, because the kiss had shaken her.

He chuckled. "So you didn't." The smile faded. "Going to stay? I'll send you back home if you really want to go."

"Oh, no, not yet," she said quickly. "We have to clear your mother first!"

He was tracing the simple silver-and-turquoise ring she wore on her right middle finger. "Did you mean what you said, about liking Tansy for a mother?"

She nodded. "I barely remember my mom. She was always away with dad somewhere. We never really knew each other. Not like I know Grandad, anyway. He's my best friend."

"I'd like to meet him when we go home," he said sincerely. "He must be one special guy."

"He is." She searched his eyes with her warm gray ones. "So are you," she added softly.

His eyes were smiling now, as well as his mouth. He looked up and down the hall and then bent and kissed her once more, briefly and tenderly. "I'll take you down to dinner when they open the restaurant," he said. "Wear something pretty."

She laughed uninhibitedly. "It'll have to be this," she indicated her beige pantsuit. "I didn't bring a dress."

He cocked an eyebrow. "Size ten?"

She gasped. "You roue!" she accused.

He shrugged. "What can I say? I spent a lot of years as a playboy. Guessing sizes is only one facet of my enormous store of knowledge." He gave her a wicked grin. "I'll have them send something over."

"Look here, you can't buy clothes for me," she said at once. "People will think I'm a kept woman!"

"Nobody, anywhere, could look at you and think that," he said flatly. "You don't have the hard edges of anybody's mistress."

"What hard edges?"

"Sophistication," he said. "It's not as alluring as the glossy magazines make it out to be. It's artificial and cold." He searched her eyes. "You're a warm, welcoming fire on a cold and rainy night."

Her eyebrows went up.

"Too corny?" he asked with a flash of white teeth. "I'll work on my approach before dinner. Consider the dress a loan, a stage prop. We wouldn't want people to think we were trailing a murderer, now would we? After all, we have no credentials and no permission to interfere in the case."

"She's your mother," she said quietly. "You have every right."

He traced her small, straight nose. "Still going to smear her in the press?"

"Don't be silly," she replied. "I only want to tell the truth."

"Your editor won't like it."

"Some editor, somewhere, will," she said. "Integrity is and should be part of every journalist's makeup. I won't slander anyone for a story."

"No wonder I like you."

He kissed the tip of her nose and sauntered off down the hall.

She watched him go with mixed emotions. She knew he'd been a playboy, that he knew all too much about women. But he was attractive and sensitive and he had a wonderful sense of humor, even though he was worried about his mother. That concern was just as alluring as his smile and charm. He really cared about Tansy, and he was willing to take chances to save her. No wonder women fell over themselves to get to him. She was on the verge of it herself.

She unlocked her door with the card key and stepped inside. And just as she closed it back again, a shadowy figure rose from the sofa in the suite's sitting room and came toward her.

Chapter 4

"Who are you?" Della asked at once, her hand still on the doorknob.

The man came closer. He had dark hair and eyes and a faintly foreign look. He tilted his head to one side and studied her, from her short, wavy blond hair to her small feet. "I'll ask the questions," he said. "Why are you looking for Tansy Deverell?"

She hesitated. "How did you know I was?"

"You arrived this morning with Christopher Deverell. I know of him, and I know his angle in this—she's his mother. I don't know yours."

"I'm a journalist," she said. "I get an exclusive interview if I can help find her."

He studied her narrowly for several seconds. "I did some research on you and Deverell before I came over. Tansy Deverell's husband—and the father of her two sons—was in Morocco during World War II," he said. "He saved the life of a young Arab who was spying for the French resistance."

"That's very interesting, but what does it have to do with Tansy?" she asked.

He moved into the light, and she could see the foreign look of him. "That young Arab was my grandfather," he said. "Ordinarily I don't get mixed up in high-profile cases, and Deverell wouldn't have had enough money to buy my help. But I'll take the case because of Deverell's father. I owe the family a favor."

"Who are you?" she asked belatedly.

"Oh, you can call me Seth," he replied carelessly.

Her eyebrows went up. "Lord Bainbridge told us about you."

"Not much, I'll wager." He moved back to the phone and with economical, graceful ease, lifted the phone and called Chris. "I'm in

Della's room," he said when Chris answered. He hung up.

It didn't take Chris two minutes to sprint the distance from his room to hers. He was admitted at once, and he gave Seth a calculating scrutiny while he held on to Della's small hand.

Seth noted the protective attitude and smiled. "She was perfectly safe," he assured Chris. "I never hurt women."

"Why did you come to her, and not to me?" Chris wanted to know.

"I don't know you personally. But I know of you," he replied with a faint smile. "And I know of your father," he replied. "He saved my father's life during World War II. Small world."

"Very," Chris agreed.

Seth moved back into the room and to a tray that was sitting on the table by the window. "I ordered high tea. Help yourselves."

They joined him at the table, warily.

He sat back with a scone in one hand and a cup of tea in the other, studying them while they sugared their own tea.

"That's bad for you," he remarked. "Sugar

is the curse of the twentieth century. Empty calories.''

''Life without sugar is no life at all,'' Della said with a grin. ''Sorry.''

He glanced at Chris as he sipped tea. ''Your mother is being held by some cronies of Tony Cartwright's,'' Seth said abruptly. ''They've got her in a garage on the Manchester road, and they've just become desperate fugitives. Lady Harvey called a press conference twenty minutes ago to publicly blame the murder on Tony, via the press camped outside her manor house. Her story is that Tony killed and robbed the old man and then planned to say she did it because her husband was going to divorce her and she'd lose her inheritance. Tony got wind of it and snatched Tansy, who has friends in high circles in Great Britain, to use as a hostage. They plan to turn her over to the police in return for an airplane to fly them out of the country.''

Chris cursed under his breath. ''Do the police know about this?''

''Not yet,'' Seth said easily. ''But they have access to the same sources I used to get the information and they'll find out what Tony's up to very shortly. Meanwhile, Lady Harvey, having freed herself from her husband and her greedy lover is busily making plans to stash her inheritance in Swiss bank accounts before it can be enjoined.''

''What about the inheritance tax? Surely she uses banks,'' Chris protested.

''She does—banks in the Bahamas. A sharp little lady, indeed, no loose ends except Tansy, and she's arranged things so that Tony will be taking care of that one.'' He finished his scone and leaned forward abruptly with the cup in his hands. ''You know they'll kill her when they get what they want, don't you? His sort doesn't take chances.''

Chris had already guessed that. His face set in grim lines. ''Damn them all,'' he said in a deep, low undertone. ''I never cheated or threatened anyone to get where I am, and I didn't inherit all that much to begin with.''

Seth nodded. ''I know.'' He pursed his lips and studied the younger man quietly. He looked hard. His eyes were like black coals. ''I can tell the police all this, including where to find Tansy, if that's what you want.''

Chris stared at him levelly. "There's an alternative," he guessed.

Seth nodded. "Myself, two men, you and Della."

Chris glanced at Della. "I'll go. She shouldn't. This isn't her fight."

She gave him her best glare. "I go," she said shortly. "It would be the best story I ever wrote!"

"Maybe the last, too," Chris said. He didn't like to think of Della in danger.

"Tell him I can go," Della said to Seth.

Seth shrugged. "You can as far as I'm concerned. You two will do my legwork for me while I set up the hit."

"You won't shoot anybody?" Della asked.

"That's up to the captors. If they shoot, we shoot back," he said with finality. "I'm not risking my men's lives."

"I thought people in England weren't allowed to carry guns," Della pointed out.

"Most people aren't. Some police and other agencies do." He met Chris's solemn gaze. "I'll clear it with the right people before I go in," he said. "I'm not an outlaw, in case that's what you were thinking. I always work within the law whenever possible. Especially in this country," he added with a smile.

"All right then. Della and I will do whatever you need. Name your price," Chris said. "I'll mortgage everything I own if that's what it takes to get Tansy back."

The other man studied him like a zoo specimen. "That's unusual these days, did you know?" he asked. "Most would rather have the money."

"Tansy's worth her weight in it," Chris said simply. "Even if she is a royal pain in the neck from time to time." He chuckled softly. "At least she's never boring."

Seth laughed. He put down his cup and stood up. "It's been a pleasure. I'll be in touch as soon as I've worked things out. Stick close to the hotel for the next day. I'll have to get a few things together and contact my men."

"Will do. But what about the payment?" Chris asked.

"The ransom, you mean?"

Chris frowned. "That, too, but I meant your fee."

"Oh, that. I'll settle for high tea at the Ritz, at your convenience," he said. "No skimping

on the cream and butter, either," he added
with a lifted finger. "First-class."

Chris looked at the man as if he were crazy.
"High tea?"

Seth shrugged. "I love high tea. I can't get
enough of it. I've already got more money than
I like to have." He glanced at Della and
smiled. "These days I take cases only when
they interest me. You're a dish."

"Thank you," she said, flushing.

He sighed. "I love blondes," he murmured.
He glanced at Chris wryly. "Pity she didn't
see me first." He nodded and went out of the
room as silently as a breath of air.

"What a very odd man," Della exclaimed
when he was gone.

"I hope we can trust him," Chris murmured. "Although I don't really see that we
have a choice. Tansy's safety has to be my first
concern."

"What do you suppose he'll ask us to do?"
she wondered.

He got up and went to the window, to stare
down at the busy street below. "At a guess,
he'll want us to go to the hideout posing as a
couple of lost tourists. It might just work.

While we've got them distracted at the front door, he and his men can go in the back.''

Della leaned forward with her forearms across her knees. ''I just can't believe people would do something this vile for money.''

''They might not, ordinarily. Lady Harvey seems to be playing both ends against the middle. No honor among thieves there, I'll wager.'' He turned back to her. ''I hate to think of Tansy in such hands.''

''I know.'' She got up and went to him, her gray eyes soft and compassionate as they met his. ''But she's been in a lot of scrapes over the years. If anyone can come out on top, it's your mother. These guys are amateurs. Your mother is a professional troublemaker.''

He forced a smile. ''Yes, she is. But this is a new kind of situation, even for her. She's diabetic,'' he added worriedly. ''I don't even know if she's got her insulin tablets with her.''

''She doesn't take insulin shots?''

He shook his head. ''For a while, she didn't even have to have pills, but she wouldn't leave sugar alone. Emotional upsets play havoc with her sugar levels, and she won't be eating properly as a captive.'' He slammed one fist into the palm of the other hand. "I'd love to get my hands on those guys for five minutes."

"We'll get her out," she said firmly. "You have to think positively."

He looked down at her through amused black eyes. "You're a tonic," he murmured. "A real tonic."

She smiled. "Thanks."

He reached out and touched her wavy blond hair lightly. "I haven't thanked you for letting me drag you into this." He was solemn all at once. "Listen, if this looks like being dangerous, I want you right out of it. I won't risk your life, even to save Tansy's."

She was taken aback by the unexpected, and touching, concern. She searched his face quietly. "You might not believe it, but I can handle myself."

"Not if you get in the way of a bullet," he assured her.

She lifted her thin eyebrows. "Have you ever been shot at?"

"Several times," he volunteered.

"In the army?"

He shook his head.

"How, then?"

"I did a brief stint as a mercenary," he confided. "Back in my wild youth, right after I got out of the service. I was in before Desert Storm. The only service I saw was in Germany, where I hit as many nightclubs as possible. After I got out, I met up with some career soldiers who were hired for a little job in Africa. I went along." He shook his head. "One taste of the life was enough to convince me it wasn't worth the price it exacted. I saw things I'll never be able to forget. When I came home, I went wild for a time. Life was suddenly short, and I was determined to squeeze every drop of pleasure out of each day."

That reminded her of the playboy he'd once been. "You didn't hold life very dear until then, did you?" she asked shrewdly.

He shrugged. "Not really," he agreed. "I didn't think very far ahead." His eyes were reflective as he stared out the window. "Looking back, it seems to me that I didn't have much grasp of the important things even after Africa. I lived from day to day and burned the candle at both ends. If it hadn't been for the wreck, I might never have strayed from that path.''

''I'm sorry it took a wreck to wake you up.''

He sighed. ''That makes two of us.'' He put his hands in his pockets and jiggled his loose change. ''Well, we seem to be stuck in the hotel tomorrow. What would you like to do to pass the time?''

''We could investigate the gym facilities,'' she offered. ''I noticed on the way down in the elevator that they have a health club for visitors here.''

''I had enough physical therapy after the wreck,'' he said. ''I'll pass.''

''They have a swimming pool,'' she said.

He looked uncomfortable. ''I don't swim.''

She glowered at him. ''You're just making up excuses. I happen to know that you swim like a fish. You spent a month at that Italian actress's villa in Rome, and you swam with her every day.''

His black eyes flashed. ''Yes. I did. That was before the wreck.''

''You mean you can't swim because of the injuries?'' she asked, puzzled.

''I can't swim because of the scars,'' he said

through his teeth. "The wreck was so bad, the car had to be cut apart to get me out." He added, "As I mentioned earlier, I had internal injuries as well as external ones, and there are gashes on my stomach and upper thigh that I don't want anyone to see."

She looked up at him quizzically. "Not even me?"

He hadn't thought about her seeing his wounds. Della wasn't like some women who would have turned away or averted her eyes. She wouldn't be intimidated by a few scars. When she looked at him, she wouldn't even see them.

"I haven't worn swimming trunks since the wreck," he murmured.

"It's time you did. A few laps in the pool will be good for you." She grinned at him. "You can teach me how to swim."

"You don't know?" he asked, aghast.

She shook her head. "There was never anyone who could teach me. Grandad can't swim, either."

"Didn't you take classes when you were in school?"

"Sure. All sorts. But not swimming."

"You should know how," he said seriously. "It might save your life one day."

"Then teach me how."

"I don't want to swim around people," he said doggedly.

"Okay. Let's wait until tonight, just at bedtime," she coaxed.

He stared at her uneasily. He didn't speak.

"Think about it," she added, and then let the subject drop.

They had a leisurely supper in the dining room. True to his word, Chris had bought her a lovely dress to wear. Della had a huge prawn cocktail, followed by Beef Wellington with exquisitely cooked vegetables and homemade breads. The dessert table was almost her undoing. She sat and stared at it for a long time before she decided what to order.

Chris watched her with undisguised delight. She ate the same way she did everything else, wholeheartedly and without inhibition. When coffee was served, she sat back with a long sigh.

"The food here is just delicious," she said fervently. "I can't remember when I've eaten anything so wonderful."

"I can't remember when I've enjoyed watching a woman eat," he murmured dryly. "Over the years, most of my dates have fancied rabbit food."

She glowered. "I'm not eating bean sprouts and tofu until I break a scale," she informed him. "Food should be a permissible vice."

"Especially at your age," he agreed with a chuckle.

"You aren't that much older than I am."

"Not chronologically," he said. "But you're a lifetime behind me in other things." He smiled with pure cynicism. "You still have illusions. I lost mine years ago."

"I hope I never do," she murmured as she toyed with her napkin. "I think that one person can make a difference in the world."

"And I know for a fact that several million people have tried and failed."

She looked up into his eyes. "How did you get so cynical?"

"I lived in the fast lane," he said with an unfamiliar hardness. "You grow up pretty fast."

She searched his black eyes curiously. "Tansy was married five times, you said."

He nodded curtly. "Our father was much older than she was. But then, Tansy was about forty when I was born. Nobody thought she could get pregnant anymore—especially Tansy."

"Was she a good mother?" she asked.

He shrugged. "She wasn't around much. When Dad was alive, I have a faint recollection of how he took her with him most places he went on business. They spent a good deal of time in Spain with his rich relatives, or in England with hers. Logan and I were pretty much raised by a succession of housekeepers and governesses."

"Is your brother like you?"

"Oh, no," he said with a smile. "Logan's the solemn one. He was always responsible and mature. I was the gadfly. Maybe that's why Tansy and I got along so well. She saw herself in me." His eyes darkened. "After Dad died, she went wild. She'd always been outgoing and cheerful, but she collected and discarded men like paper napkins. After she divorced the last one, she seemed to enjoy creating scandals. Not that I can throw stones," he added in a soft, sensual tone. "I've done my share of headlining."

"She must have cared for your father a great deal," Della observed.

He frowned and then laughed hollowly. "Amazing that you knew that at once. It took me years to work it out."

It occurred to her belatedly that many of his stepfathers might not have liked a ready-made family. "Those stepfathers, were they very hard to take?"

He nodded. "For me, more than for Logan. By the time Tansy remarried, Logan was out on his own. I wasn't. Eventually Tansy decided that a military school would be just what the doctor ordered. I liked it, but I resented Tansy too much to stay there. I jumped ship after the first year and ended up in Spain with one of my father's brothers. Tansy let me alone. Eventually I wandered back to the States, just in time to register for the draft. By then, the military seemed as good a choice as any, so I enlisted."

"Nobody can say your life hasn't been interesting," she pointed out.

He chuckled. "It's been useless, for the

most part,'' he replied. "Just lately, I've been feeling my age. Making money is nice, but I want to do something else." His eyes held a faraway look. "I want to build yachts. Racing yachts. It's been a dream of mine for years, but I've never had the commitment to try it. After spending time in Spain this summer, I've almost come to a decision. My friend who races in the America's Cup competitions has offered to go into partnership with me. I'm very tempted."

"You should follow your dreams," she said seriously.

He searched her face. "Do you know, I'm beginning to think I have a few of them left."

She smiled. "I'm glad."

The pool, as Della had guessed, was deserted late at night. Since Chris didn't have swimming trunks, he had to buy a pair—but they were conservative, black with white stripes and as long as boxer shorts. Despite the scars that he was so self-conscious about, he looked good in trunks. His natural olive tan made his eyes and hair look even darker than they were, and his body was muscular without being exaggerated. Della found him exciting and had to force herself not to stare.

She was wearing a one-piece canary yellow suit that outlined her hourglass figure very well.

"Not bad, Miss Larson," Chris drawled, giving her a sensual appraisal that made her knees feel weak. "Not bad at all."

"I could say the same thing," she murmured with a shy smile.

He moved closer, so that she could see the thin white scars that crisscrossed his abdomen and what she could see of his thighs. "Could you?" he asked with faint cynicism.

"If you think a few scars would put women off you, you're nuts," she said flatly. "You're devastating."

He chuckled. "Plain speaking, and here I thought you were shy."

"I am, mostly. But you're creating a problem that doesn't exist," she added. "The scars have faded so much that you have to look close to see them." She searched his eyes. "And it isn't noticeable that you only have vision in one eye," she murmured. "I'm sorry about the wreck. But you're still the man you were, aren't you?''

He moved even closer. ''Am I? Let's see.''

Before she could decide whether or not he was teasing, he bent and lifted her off the tile floor, holding her close to his warm body.

She gripped his shoulders hard. ''You aren't going to toss me in?'' she asked worriedly as he moved closer to the edge.

''I was thinking about it,'' he confessed.

''I'm afraid of deep water,'' she told him.

''Okay.'' He put her down at the steps that led into the shallow end of the pool. ''Go at your own speed.''

She smiled. ''Thanks.''

She eased down into the cool water, feeling it absorb her like wet silk. She sighed and spread her arms, enjoying the feel of it, but still on her feet.

Chris moved close to her and lifted her arms around his neck. ''I won't let you drown,'' he promised, and struck off to the deeper water. ''You're an elemental person, aren't you?'' he asked quietly. ''You're sensual.''

She laughed nervously. ''I've never been called that before!''

He didn't smile. His eyes were locked with hers as he paused at shoulder depth, holding her lightly by the waist so she didn't sink. ''I'm sure you've never given yourself much opportunity to find out. It's pure loss of control to let your senses go free.'' He brought her close. ''But it's time you learned how sweet it is.''

''I don't...''

His mouth covered hers, stopping the words in the back of her throat. She'd been kissed before, but Chris was a totally new experience. He nibbled at her lips, teased them with his tongue, savored them until they parted and began to respond shyly to the lazy insistence of his warm, hard mouth.

She made a feeble effort to save herself, pushing gently at his broad shoulders, but he didn't stop. If anything, he became more demanding. On a soft, harsh groan, his hands went down to her hips and pressed them firmly into the aroused contours of his own. He held the kiss, built it into something devouring and frightening.

Della cried out softly as his hands became

invasive, teasing under the elastic at her legs to find the soft skin of her thighs and hips.

He lifted his mouth. His eyes were black and his breathing wasn't quite normal. His hands lifted from her thighs, but they slid up and kept going until they found and caressed her high, firm breasts.

"Chris…!" she choked.

His thumb and forefinger tested the hardness of a small nipple while he searched her shocked eyes. He bent and kissed her at the same time that his hand slid inside the deep V of the bathing suit and found soft bare skin. His other arm impelled her even closer to his aroused body.

Della was flying. She knew that if she lived to be a hundred, there would never be another moment like this, another man like this. He was experienced, but it wasn't his way with women that attracted her. It was everything about him.

The sound of voices broke them reluctantly apart. He moved his hands back discreetly to her waist and held her there, fighting for breath, as a party of people came out to the pool area and put down towels and drinks on nearby tables.

"What will you do," he asked softly, "if I suggest that we go back to my room and finish what we started?"

She smiled. "I'd suggest that you teach me how to swim instead."

He chuckled. "As I suspected. Well, dash my dreams to bits, why don't you?" he murmured. "I'll never sleep."

"You will if you're tired enough," she assured him. She moved back a little. "Come on. Teach me."

"This isn't what I want to teach you, you little blond witch," he muttered.

She grinned. "Sure it is! Just think, I might make it to the Olympics, and you could tell everyone that you taught me everything I know."

He let out a long, wistful sigh. "Okay, you win." He shook his head as he looked at her. "What raw potential."

She made a face at him. "Swimming. Teach me swimming."

"Would you believe that you're the first woman who ever turned me down flat?"

"There's a first time for everything," she assured him.

He shook his head and moved her into a position on her back. "We'll begin with floating," he said. "This will give you confidence in the water."

It didn't, at first. But as they went along, she began to feel less intimidated by the deep water beneath her. The pool was lighted, and there were lamps on long poles all the way around it. Chris seemed both relaxed and pleased with her company. A gorgeous brunette in the party of people nearby found him attractive and tried to flirt with him. To Della's surprise, he cut her off abruptly and in such a way that she didn't try it again.

As they were going up in the elevator to their rooms, Della studied him from the folds of her beach robe with curious eyes.

"She was gorgeous, you know," she told him.

He searched her eyes. "You're gorgeous," he replied, and he wasn't teasing. "Inside and out. After you, I don't know that I could look at another woman."

She caught her breath. "Isn't this sudden?"

He nodded. "Like lightning striking. You never see it coming. Then it hits, and your life changes."

"Changes, how?" she asked hesitantly.

"I'm not sure yet." He studied her oval face quietly. "I wouldn't have gone into the water if you hadn't insisted," he said. "I'm glad you did. I don't look as bad as I thought, apparently."

"Of course you don't," she scoffed. "You're still devastating to women, scars and all."

"I noticed," he replied with a speaking glance at her body.

She felt uneasy. "You aren't angry?"

His eyebrows lifted. "At what?"

"At me, for not wanting to go back to your room with you."

He only smiled. "I'm disappointed. I'm not angry." The elevator stopped and he caught her hand in his and held it until they reached her door. He turned to face her after she'd inserted the card key and opened it. "I like you the way you are, Della," he said. "Old-fashioned hang-ups and all."

"I'm glad."

He bent and kissed her gently. "Get some sleep. I have a feeling we're going headfirst into the fire in the morning."

"You, too," she said. She reached up and brushed back a lock of unruly dark hair from his forehead. Her heart was in her eyes. "You need someone to take care of you," she said quietly. "You don't take care of yourself."

His fingers touched her cheek. "You might take on the job," he said softly. "There's a vacancy."

She smiled. "I'll think about it. Good night. Sleep well."

"You, too."

He gave her a long last look before he wandered off down the hall in his own beach robe, looking as elegant as he did in a suit. Della watched him until he was out of sight. It occurred to her that she was in love with him.

Chapter 5

The day dawned rainy and dreary. Della ordered breakfast from room service and sat down by herself to eat it. She was still elated from the night before and anxious to see Chris, to see if he regretted how far things had gone between them.

He rang the bell just as she was drinking a second cup of coffee. She went to let him in. His dark eyes approved the soft yellow suit she was wearing with a lacy white blouse and white high heels.

"You look elegant," he mused.

She liked the way he looked in slacks and a navy jacket with a roll-neck sweater. "So do you," she replied.

He closed the door behind him and pulled her close, bending to kiss her with tender warmth. "Good morning," he whispered.

"Good morning." She pulled his head down and kissed him back, melting into his tall, hard body with obvious pleasure.

"Morning is always the best time," he murmured against her mouth.

"Is it, really?"

He wrapped her up against him, loving the smallness of her in his arms, the way she clung to him. "I've avoided commitment all my life," he said at her ear. "Trust me to let a gorgeous little blonde waltz up on my blind side."

"I'm not gorgeous."

"You're gorgeous." He held her closer. "Don't think you're going to get rid of me when this is all over," he remarked, feeling her heart jump at the statement. "I'll be tenacious."

"What a lovely thought," she purred.

He drew in a long breath. "I suppose it will

have to be orange blossoms and white lace, after all," he said. "You'll be a vision in white."

"Are you proposing?" she squeaked.

"Of course."

She drew back. "We don't know each other!"

"We'll get married and go from there." He searched her soft eyes. "We like each other, we're attracted to each other, and we have mutual elderly headaches to take care of." He shrugged. "It's more than a lot of couples have to start with. Where's your sense of adventure? Don't you ever take risks?"

She was floored. She'd expected anything from him except a proposal. "You've had so many women in your life..."

"And now I only want one. You." He was dead serious. "We'll go at your pace. But at the end of the road, there's going to be orange blossoms and lace. Period."

She smiled slowly, feeling as if fountains of joy were rising up into her heart. "I can't believe it."

"Neither can I," he chuckled. "But there it

is. All we have to do is rescue Tansy and get on with it."

Her face fell. "How can I possibly interview my future mother-in-law for a scoop?" she asked suddenly, horrified.

"You'll be kind to her," he said simply. "You're the very best person to do it." He sighed. "God, I hope she's all right. I hardly slept, worrying about her."

Just as he finished the statement, the telephone rang. He went past Della to pick it up. He listened carefully, murmured something, and hung up.

"Seth," he explained when she looked the question at him. "I've got an address. We're honeymooners, lost and looking for directions." He grinned. "I told you I know how mercenaries work." The smile faded. "You do exactly as I say. I won't risk you, not even for Tansy."

She nuzzled against him for a few sweet seconds. "I won't risk you, either," she said softly. "Let's hope Seth knows what he's doing."

"Amen!"

* * *

The address was on the outskirts of London in what looked to be a shabby apartment house. Chris took Della firmly by the hand and moved to the front door. There was a doorbell. He rang it. There was no answer. He looked at Della, concerned, and rang it again.

The door suddenly opened. A young man in a leather jacket peered at them from behind it. "What yer want?" he demanded.

Chris drew Della closer. "We're from America," he drawled. "Just got in from the airport and we're lost. Trying to find a cousin of ours, a...wait a sec." He drew a piece of paper from his pocket and read, "Billy Withers, 44 Truebridge Lane, London." He looked around. "This is Truebridge, but we can't find number 44."

The man looked irritated and impatient. "T'ain't no such number!"

Chris's face fell. "But we've come all this way! Are you sure you have no idea?"

There was a crashing sound in the back of the apartment. The young man scowled, turning toward the inside of the dark room. His hand went to his jacket.

Della never saw Chris move, but the next

minute, the young man was on the floor and Chris was standing over him with an automatic weapon. He cocked it with confident ease and leveled it at the downed man.

"Seth!" he called loudly.

There was another scuffle, another crash, and a familiar face appeared in the hall.

"Damn!" Seth exclaimed when he saw the man on the floor. "That was a neat piece of work," he murmured, grinning as he bent to drag the young man up from the floor. "Come along, Tansy's in here."

"Is she all right?" Chris asked quickly, drawing Della's cold hand into his free one.

"She's a little rocky, but I gave her a pack of glucose. She's rallying."

Tansy was sitting on the edge of a ragged little cot, sucking on a glucose packet, looking weary and almost defeated. She looked up and saw Chris and burst into tears.

Chris put the safety on the pistol and tossed it to one of Seth's men before he bent and gathered Tansy close.

"You idiot!" he muttered at her ear, holding her closer. "Dear God, you gave us a scare!"

"Which is nothing compared to what I got, my dear," Tansy sighed, clinging to her son. "My globe-trotting days are over. This is the absolute end." She lifted her head. "Did they find poor Cecil?"

"Yes, just after you vanished. Have you been here the whole time?" Chris asked.

She nodded. "They snatched me and held me until they got their money from Lady Harvey. I was a material witness and she told them to keep me here for collateral until she could get to her funds." She laughed hollowly. "I gather from what those goons said that she reneged and expected them to finish me off. They decided it might be better to hold on to me, because I could implicate her. She doesn't know that," she added. "But I was wearing a wire when she confessed that she and Tony Cartwright had planned Cecil's death."

Seth was suddenly all business. "What happened to the recording?"

"He had it." She pointed to the man on the floor.

Seth pulled out a nasty-looking knife. "Get them out of here," he told Chris.

Chris moved the women ahead of him and

looked back at the nervous man on the floor, presumably the vile Tony. "He usually only takes a finger. For his collection," he added with a cold smile. "In your case, it might be an organ. A vital organ. If I were you, I'd tell him what he wants to know. In any case, I'll remove the ladies before you start screaming."

They were in the next room with the door closed before Tansy turned to him. "You enjoyed that," she accused.

He smiled grimly. "Yes, I did. After what he put you through, I'd have enjoyed slugging him even more, but I think our friend Seth will do what's necessary."

"Lord Bainbridge, you mean," she corrected.

"We met Lord Bainbridge," Chris said carefully. "He's seventy."

"He's sixty-five," Tansy stated. She jerked her head toward the door. "That's his son—his only son—a colonel in the SAS until he retired year before last. Now he's what the secret agencies call a problem-solver. Thank God he came after me. I don't think I could have made it another day. I'm so weak, son."

"We'll get you to a hospital and have you checked over, just to be safe," Chris said.

Tansy was staring past him at the pretty little blonde. "Who's this?"

"Della Larson," he introduced. "She's eventually going to be your daughter-in-law when she makes up her mind that I'm serious about marrying her. But for the meantime, she's a reporter. I promised her an exclusive interview if she came with me to find you."

"She came right in here with you?" Tansy pursed her lips. She was impressed. "Brave girl."

Della grinned. "That makes several of us. I'm glad to meet you, Mrs. Deverell, and I'm very glad that we got here in time!"

Tansy shook the hand that was offered and smiled broadly. "So am I, dear." She lifted both eyebrows. "You're going to marry my son, are you?"

Della sighed. "I think so," she mused. "Of course, he may change his mind now that we're all out of danger."

"He won't," Chris drawled.

"He's my son," Tansy said. "I taught him always to do what he said he would." She seemed to slump. "I want a steak," she said. "And French fries and cherry cobbler and..."

"No cherry cobbler," Chris informed her.

She made a face at him. "Even the most rigid diet allows sweets occasionally."

"Not yours."

"Just wait..."

Chris put an arm around her and drew her close. "You can have mangoes and bananas and coconut."

She sighed. "My dear, you remembered!"

"How could I forget? The kitchen was always cluttered with mangoes," he told Della. "She likes desserts, but fruit was always her favorite." He glared at Tansy. "This time, you're going where you can be found. No more adventures."

"Spoilsport!"

"You could have died," he retorted.

"Eventually we all do." She shook her head. "Poor Cecil. He and I were friends years ago. He wrote to me and invited me to visit. I hadn't met his new wife, so I accepted. But after I'd been there for a few days, I realized that not only did his wife not love him, but she was obsessed with getting her hands on the estate. He vanished one night, just after that shady man in there—'' her head jerked toward the closed door ''—came to visit Lady Harvey. She woke me the next morning and said that Cecil was dead and I was the prime suspect, because his will named me as executrix and chief beneficiary. Lies, of course, but I was too stunned to question her. Tony Cartwright hustled me out the door and into his car, and said he'd hide me. But that wasn't what he did. He and his cronies brought me here and held chloroform to my nose and mouth. When I woke up, I was locked in that room.'' She smiled wearily. ''I thought I'd never get out alive. I heard them discussing what to do to me after her ladyship went public and accused Tony of killing her husband. He'll be the prosecution's best witness at her trial, unless I miss my guess.''

''Not without that tape recording he won't,'' Chris said solemnly. ''Speaking of which...''

He turned toward the door just as Seth came out, all dressed in black, with cold eyes. He had something in his hand—a tiny tape recorder.

''The evidence!'' Tansy exclaimed.

Seth nodded. "Irrefutable. Tony's decided to become the state's own witness. One of my men is telephoning the police even as we speak. I'm going to slip out with my men before they get here." He put a heavy hand on Chris's shoulder. "You're a hero. I'm proud of you."

"I didn't do anything except disarm one of the henchmen," Chris argued.

"Well, I sure as hell didn't do anything," Seth remarked haughtily. "I wouldn't soil my hands with such filth."

Tansy went to Seth, stood on tiptoe, and kissed his lean cheek. "Thank you, dear."

He kissed her back and smiled warmly. "Come visiting again. But do it in a conventional way this time, hmm?"

"Behave yourself," Tansy directed.

"I'm the soul of discretion," Seth assured her. He grinned at Della, glanced at Chris, and suddenly caught Della around the waist, bent her back over his arm, and kissed her with exaggerated passion.

He let her up, breathless and flushed, and grinned wickedly. "You should have met me first," he repeated. He waved at the others, went to gather his men, and went stealthily out the back door.

"Damned bounder," Chris muttered, staring at Della.

"Don't you worry," Della assured him as she smoothed down her hair. "He's very good—but you're better."

Chris's expression lightened. "Am I?"

She grinned. "Much."

Tansy burst out laughing. "And that answers that question, doesn't it, my boy?" she asked her son.

"Yes," he agreed with a warm smile. "I suppose it does."

They gave the tape recorder and the men over to the police when they arrived and gave statements as well. Tansy was taken to the hospital to be checked over. They kept her overnight and Della stayed in the room with her while Chris wound up the details of their trip, returned the rental car, and got Tansy a seat on their flight back to Texas.

"It's been a very exciting trip," Della told the older woman, "although I'm sorry for what you went through."

"It was an adventure, and it will improve with every retelling," Tansy assured her with a wicked chuckle. "You and I are going to get along very well, my dear. I can tell that we're the same sort of people."

"Well, not exactly. But you should meet my grandfather," she told the older woman. "He was a war correspondent."

"War correspondent?" Tansy frowned. "Your last name is Larson? Is your grandfather Herbert Larson of UPI?"

Della blinked. "Well, yes."

"For heaven's sake!"

"You couldn't...you don't know him?" Della asked.

"Know him!" Tansy caught her breath and laid back among the pillows. "I'm surprised that he's still alive, the chances he used to take!"

"You *do* know him!" Della exclaimed.

"About forty years ago," Tansy said, "he and I were pinned down by Latin American revolutionaries when I was in South America, just after my first husband's death. Your grandfather got me to the airport and onto a plane bound for home. I never met a man with such grit, such fire. He was…superb.''

Della smiled. "He still is. He doesn't get around as well, and his sight isn't what it should be, but he's kicking." She hesitated. "He's diabetic but he won't give up sweets. That sounds familiar, too, doesn't it?" she added.

Tansy flushed. "Well, well."

"He and I live together," Della continued. She stopped dead and frowned. "Oh, dear."

"Oh, dear, what?"

"I can't leave him," she said plaintively, staring at Tansy with huge worried gray eyes. "He'll die if I'm not there to make him take his medicine and keep him away from the sugar bowl!"

Tansy reached over and patted her hand where it lay on the coverlet. "You marry Chris," she said firmly. "And let me worry about Herbert. I think I may have a solution to your problem."

Della didn't believe her. But when they arrived back in the States, and found Herbert Larson sitting in a seat next to the concourse entrance at the Houston airport, she began to understand what Tansy meant.

The old man, silver haired and dignified, rose as the travelers came out of the airplane down to the concourse in the covered tunnel. He opened his arms and a happy Della ran into them to be hugged firmly and kissed. Tansy came out of the tunnel after her and stopped as the elderly man let go of Della and stood just looking at her. She was holding on to Chris's arm, but she let it go and moved slowly toward the elderly man.

They just looked at each other for a long moment. "You've got wrinkles," Herbert said abruptly.

"You've got flat feet," Tansy shot back.

"My granddaughter says she's going to marry your son."

"Too bad if you don't like it," Tansy said huffily.

He shrugged. "Looks like a nice boy," he mused, glancing at Chris with a faint smile. "I like it. Della needs looking after. She's too soft to be a reporter."

"She's not too soft to be a political featurist,'' Tansy said firmly. "It's what she likes to do best.''

"She'll enjoy having kids and raising them more,'' Herbert Larson said. "She's a home-body, like my late wife was. No traipsing around the world getting into scrapes for Martha, no sir!''

"Well, let's hear it for Saint Martha!'' Tansy said through her teeth.

Herbert raised an eyebrow and studied her closely. "Still jealous after forty years, hmm?'' he taunted.

"Della says you won't give up sugar,'' Tansy remarked, ignoring his question.

"She says the same thing about you. Trying to die?'' he accused bluntly.

Tansy went scarlet. "I could ask you the same question!''

He shrugged thin shoulders. "I thought about it. Not anymore, though.'' His eyes narrowed. "I've just found a new lease on life. You like nightclubs?''

She nodded jerkily.

"Dancing?''

She nodded again.

He pursed his lips. "Maybe I'll give you a

whirl, if you play your cards right. You never could do a tango.''

''And you can?''

''I taught Valentino how,'' he bragged.

''You were in short pants when Valentino died,'' she accused.

''If I'd been old enough, I'd have taught him how,'' he said with a grin. He went forward and took her arm. ''Come on, Grandma. I'll help you out to the car.''

''You can drive?'' she asked mockingly.

''No, but I hired a man who could. Nothing's too good for my granddaughter.''

They walked ahead of the others, still arguing. Chris drew Della close to his side as they walked, pulling luggage on wheels behind them.

''I think some of our problems are about to be solved. Apparently, they know each other.''

Della nodded. ''And fairly well, from the look of things. Miracles never cease.''

''I hope they won't kill each other before we get married.''

She chuckled. ''Oh, I don't think there's much danger of that.'' She slid her hand into his and looked up at him with her whole heart in her soft gray eyes. "I can't wait to marry you," she added in a breathless whisper.

He squeezed her hand, hard. His dark eyes were expressive on her face. "Neither can I." He hesitated. "You don't mind the scars?"

She smiled and pressed close against his side. "Don't be silly."

His eyes closed briefly and his arm went around her, contracting almost painfully. It was like having every single dream of happiness he'd ever had come true. He could hardly contain the feeling it gave him to know she loved him.

"I love you, Della," he said tautly.

She looked up into eyes that adored her. "I love you, too." She smiled impishly. "How soon can we get married?"

He searched her soft features warmly. "As soon as I can get a license. You're not about to get away from me!"

They were married by a justice of the peace exactly three days later, with Tansy and Herbert for witnesses. The elderly couple were holding hands, apparently having decided that fighting was less fun than exploring each others' personalities. In a relatively short time, they'd rediscovered the feelings they had for each other years ago, and they were inseparable.

Chris and Della drove them back to Herbert's apartment before they drove to the airport to catch their plane to Spain. They were going to Malaga, on the southern shores of Spain, along the Costa del Sol, for an extended honeymoon. Della, who'd traveled little in her life, was exuberant about the adventure of it. She couldn't wait to get there.

When they arrived and passed through customs, they took a cab to their hotel overlooking the blistering white beach and blue sea. The hotel was white stucco with gardens full of blossoming flowers. It was a dream of a place, with wrought-iron balconies and the smell of the sea air fresh and clean.

"The Rock of Gibraltar is very close by," Chris told her when they were installed in their suite, "and so is Morocco. We might take a day trip over there and explore the souq—the marketplace."

She turned from the window that led out to the balcony and stared at him hungrily, drinking in the sight of his long, lean body in white slacks and a red designer knit shirt. She was wearing a loose, comfortable crinkly cotton dress with tiny shoulder bows and little beneath it, because of the heat.

"Alone at last," she said with a soft smile. Her hands went to the shoulder bows and slowly undid them, letting the dress fall to the floor. Under it, she wore a white lace teddy that emphasized every sweet curve of her young body.

Chris caught his breath. He went to her, his hands slow and caressing on her shoulders. "You don't want supper first?" he asked quietly.

She shook her head. Her arms went up and around his neck. "I want you first," she whispered, and drew his mouth down on hers.

The passion was explosive. She'd dreamed of being in his arms without fabric between them, and here it was happening, so naturally that she never thought to feel embarrassed. He eased her out of her clothing between soft, brief kisses that traveled the length of her body, each one more sensual and arousing than the one before.

She knew that he was experienced, but until now she had no knowledge of the reality of intimacy. He aroused her expertly, slowly, taking his time, soothing all her secret fears until she was dazed and shivering with the pleasure he gave her.

By the time he drew her carefully under him and eased down, she was eager and totally without fear or reserve. She lifted to meet the slow, sensuous downward thrust of his hips and laughed with pure pleasure when the tiny flash of pain was experienced and abruptly replaced by delicious sensations that rippled over her like waves.

His lean hands moved her, teased her, taught her, while his mouth devoured hers in the stillness of the cool room. There was a rhythm that she hadn't expected. It built the new sensations she was feeling into torrential spasms of pleasure that overwhelmed her unexpectedly and lifted her against him in a fever of submission.

She hid her face in his hot throat as the spasms broke against themselves, twisting her under his demanding body as she reached and reached and finally found the exquisite source of the tiny sips of fulfillment she'd only sampled.

He felt her go rigid, and at once, he drove for his own satisfaction, his mouth hard against her breast as he soared into the heights with her.

When he collapsed at her side, she was still shivering, and laughing through the little aftershocks of ecstasy that left her moving restlessly on the bed.

"So it's like that," she whispered, awed.

"It's like that," he whispered back. He smiled and rolled over, his face damp with sweat, his eyes blazing with love. "Was I worth waiting for? You certainly were!"

She chuckled and drew him down, so that she could kiss him with lazy enthusiasm. "Yes, you were," she murmured. "I'm sleepy."

"So am I. We'll have a nice nap and then we'll go and find the nearest seafood bar."

"I love seafood," she murmured drowsily.

"Me, too."

He drew her close at his side and pulled the sheet over them, because the room was cooling. His last thought as he slid into oblivion was that a lifetime of Della wasn't going to be quite enough...

They called Tansy and Herbert the next morning to enthuse about the sights and sounds of Spain.

"I'm glad you two are having fun," Tansy said with laughter in her voice. "When you come home, we'll have another wedding."

"What?" Chris burst out.

"Herbert proposed," Tansy said. "And *this* time, I accepted."

He handed the phone to Della. "You aren't going to believe this," he told her.

"What?" she exclaimed when her grandfather told her the news.

"Haven't you people ever heard that you can marry more than once?" Herbert asked with disgust. "For heaven's sake, she's a dish. No way am I letting her get away from me now!"

"Well, congratulations, Grandad," Della said with love in her voice. "I couldn't be more pleased."

"Neither could I," Chris said loudly.

"You two enjoy yourselves. Tansy knows

this little Japanese place downtown where they have that strange fish. Can't think what it's called. Anyway we're going there for a snack. You kids have fun. Talk to you soon. Bye!''

He hung up. Della glanced at her husband with a frown. "They're going to a Japanese place to have a strange fish."

Chris went pale. "Not fugu. Please. Tell me it's not fugu."

"What's a fugu?"

He grabbed up the receiver and placed a call to Tansy's apartment. Herbert answered.

"If you eat a fugu fish, I'll hire a man to do nothing but follow the two of you around, full-time, I swear it!" Chris said harshly.

"Fugu? Are you daft, son?" Herbert sighed. "Tansy, what's the name of that fish?"

"Sushimi," she called back.

Chris went red. "Oh," he said.

"Fugu, indeed. He thought we were going to eat fugu fish!" he called to Tansy.

"He's on his honeymoon, Herb, what do you expect? Now hang up and come help me get into this dress. We'll be late for our reservation!"

Chris laughed until Della was worried about

him. When he told her what was going on at the apartment, she only grinned.

"They'll be happy together," she said.

"Each of them alone is a handful. Can you possibly imagine what it's going to be like to have *two* of them conspiring?"

Della grimaced. "I hadn't thought about that."

"Well, don't. Not now, anyway." He picked her up and kissed her gently. "We have six days of our honeymoon left, and we're not wasting a minute worrying about them."

"What are we going to do, then?" she whispered wickedly.

He chuckled as he turned toward the bed. "I'm glad you asked…"

So was she.

*   *   *   *   *

In December 1999,
Mira Books presents

PAPER ROSE

by bestselling author

Diana Palmer

Tate had come to her rescue in her teens, a bold and strong hero. Now Cecily was a woman on her way to a brilliant career, but Tate still thought of her as a girl who needed protecting. Her love for him was a paper rose, which longed for the magic to make it real.

Now a political scandal has an unknowing Tate caught in the middle, and it is Cecily who must come, secretly, to *his* rescue and protect him from a secret which could destroy his life. And in the process, her paper rose has a chance to become real....

Just turn the page for an exciting preview of PAPER ROSE.

Chapter One

In the crowded airport in Tulsa, Cecily Blake juggled her carry-on bag with a duffel bag full of equipment, scanning the milling rush around her for Tate Winthrop. She was wearing her usual field gear: boots, a khaki suit with a safari jacket. Her natural platinum blond hair was in a neat braided bun atop her head, and through her glasses with large lenses, her pale-green eyes twinkled with anticipation. It wasn't often that Tate Winthrop asked her to help him on a case. It was an occasion.

Suddenly, there he was, towering over the

people around him. He was Lakota Sioux, and looked it. He had high cheekbones and big black, deep-set eyes under a jutting brow. His mouth was wide and sexy, with a thin upper lip and a chiseled lower one, with perfect teeth. His hair was straight and jet-black. He was lean and striking, muscular without being obvious. And he'd once worked for a very secret government agency. Of course, Cecily wasn't supposed to know that—or that he was consulting with them on the sly right now in a hush-hush murder case in Oklahoma.

"Where's your luggage?" Tate asked in his deep, crisp voice.

She gave him a pert look, taking in the elegance of his vested suit. "Where's your field gear?" she countered with the ease of long acquaintance.

Tate had saved her from the unsavory advances of a drunken stepfather when she was just seventeen. He'd been her guardian angel through four years of college and the master's program she was beginning now—doing forensic archaeology. She was already earning respect for her work. She was an honors student all the way, not surprising since she had eyes for no man in the world except Tate.

"I'm security chief of the Hutton corporation," he reminded her. "This is a freelance favor I'm doing for a couple of old friends. So this *is* my working gear."

"You'll get all dusty."

He made a deep sound in his throat. "You can brush me off."

Her eyes lit up and she grinned wickedly. "Now that's what I call incentive!"

"Cut it out. We've got a serious and sensitive situation here."

"So you intimated on the phone. What do you want me to do out here?" she asked, sounding like the professional she was. "You mentioned something about skeletal remains."

He looked around her stealthily. "We had a tip that a murder could be solved if we looked in a certain place. About twenty years ago, a foreign double agent went missing near Tulsa. He was carrying a piece of microfilm that identified a mole in the CIA. It would be embarrassing for everybody if this is him and the microfilm surfaced now."

"I gather that your mole has moved up in the world?"

"Don't even ask," he told her. "All you have to do is tell me if this DB is the one we're looking for."

"Dead body," she translated, then frowned. "I thought you had an expert out here."

"You can't imagine what sort of expert these guys brought with them. Besides," he added with a quick glance, "you're a clam. I know from experience that you don't tell everything you know."

"What did your expert tell you about the body?"

"That it's very old," he said with exaggerated awe. "Probably thousands of years old!"

"Why do you think it isn't?"

"For one thing, there's a .32 caliber bullet in the skull."

"Well, that rather lets out a Paleo-Indian hunter," she agreed.

"Sure it does. But I need an expert to say so, or the case will be summarily dropped."

"You do realize that somebody could have been out to the site and used the skull for target practice?"

He nodded. "Can you date the remains?"

"I'll do the best I can."

"That's good enough for me. You're the only person I could think of to call."

"I'm flattered."

"You're good," he said. "That's not flattery."

"When do we leave for the site?" she asked.

"Right now."

After they retrieved her luggage from the baggage claim, he led the way to a big black sport utility vehicle. He put her bags in the back and opened the door for her. She wasn't beautiful, but she had a way about her. She was intelligent, lively, outrageous and she made him feel good inside. She could have become his world, if he'd allowed her to. But he was a full-blooded Lakota, and she was not. If he ever married, something his profession made unlikely, he didn't like the idea of mixed blood.

He got in beside her and impatiently reached for her seat belt, snapping it in place. "You always forget," he murmured, meeting her eyes.

Her breath came uneasily through her lips as she met the level stare and responded helplessly to it. He was handsome and sexy and she loved him more than her own life. She had for years. But it was a hopeless, unreturned adoration that left her unfulfilled. He'd never touched her, not even in the most innocent way. He only looked.

"I should close my door to you," she said huskily. "Refuse to speak to you, refuse to see you, and get on with my life. You're a constant torment."

Unexpectedly, he reached out and touched her soft cheek with just his fingertips. They smoothed down to her full, soft mouth and teased the lower lip away from the upper one. "I'm Lakota," he said quietly. "You're white."

"There is," she said unsteadily, "such a thing as birth control."

His face was very solemn and his eyes were narrow and intent on hers. "And sex is all you want from me, Cecily?" he said mockingly. "No kids, ever?"

She couldn't look away from his dark eyes.

She wanted him. But she wanted children, too, eventually. Her expression told him so.

"Cecily, what you really want I can't give you. We have no future together. If I marry one day, it's important to me that I marry a woman with the same background as my own. I don't want to live with a young, and all too innocent, white woman."

"I wouldn't be innocent if you'd cooperate for an hour," she muttered outrageously.

He chuckled. "Under different circumstances, I would," he said, and there was suddenly something hot and dangerous in the way he looked at her as the smile faded from his lips, something that made her heart race even faster. "You tempt me too often. This teasing is more dangerous than you realize."

She didn't reply. She couldn't. She was throbbing, aroused, sick with desire. In all her life, there had been only this man who made her feel alive, who made her feel passion. Despite the traumatic experience of her teens, she had a fierce connection to Tate that she was incapable of feeling with anyone else.

Coming this September 1999 from SILHOUETTE BOOKS and bestselling author

RACHEL LEE

CONARD COUNTY:
Boots & Badges

Alicia Dreyfus—a desperate woman on the run— is about to discover that she *can* come home again...to Conard County. Along the way she meets the man of her dreams—and brings together three other couples, whose love blossoms beneath the bold Wyoming sky.

Enjoy four complete, **brand-new** stories in one extraordinary volume.

Available at your favorite retail outlet.

If you enjoyed what you just read,
then we've got an offer you can't resist!

Take 2 bestselling love stories FREE!

Plus get a FREE surprise gift!

Clip this page and mail it to Silhouette Reader Service™

IN U.S.A.	**IN CANADA**
3010 Walden Ave.	P.O. Box 609
P.O. Box 1867	Fort Erie, Ontario
Buffalo, N.Y. 14240-1867	L2A 5X3

YES! Please send me 2 free Silhouette Romance® novels and my free surprise gift. Then send me 6 brand-new novels every month, which I will receive months before they're available in stores. In the U.S.A., bill me at the bargain price of $2.90 plus 25¢ delivery per book and applicable sales tax, if any*. In Canada, bill me at the bargain price of $3.25 plus 25¢ delivery per book and applicable taxes**. That's the complete price and a savings of over 10% off the cover prices—what a great deal! I understand that accepting the 2 free books and gift places me under no obligation ever to buy any books. I can always return a shipment and cancel at any time. Even if I never buy another book from Silhouette, the 2 free books and gift are mine to keep forever. So why not take us up on our invitation. You'll be glad you did!

215 SEN CNE7
315 SEN CNE9

Name	(PLEASE PRINT)	
Address	Apt.#	
City	State/Prov.	Zip/Postal Code

* Terms and prices subject to change without notice. Sales tax applicable in N.Y.
** Canadian residents will be charged applicable provincial taxes and GST.
All orders subject to approval. Offer limited to one per household.
® are registered trademarks of Harlequin Enterprises Limited.

SROM99   ©1998 Harlequin Enterprises Limited

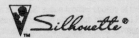

New York Times Bestselling Author

DIANA PALMER

Maggie Turner returned to her Texas hometown with her daughter, seeking comfort and safety. Instead she found sexy, dangerous Gabe Coleman. *Ten years* Maggie had been gone, and Gabe was still cold and distant...still irresistible. Maggie thought marriage had cured her of desire. Then the raging passion of a Texas cowboy taught her about love.

RAGE OF
Passion

"Nobody tops Diana Palmer."—Jayne Ann Krentz

On sale mid-August 1999 wherever paperbacks are sold!

MIRA

Silhouette ROMANCE™

VIRGIN BRIDES

Your favorite authors
tell more heartwarming
stories of lovely brides
who discover love...
for the first time....

July 1999 GLASS SLIPPER BRIDE
Arlene James (SR #1379)
Bodyguard Jack Keller had to protect innocent
Jillian Waltham—day and night. But when his assignment
became a matter of temporary marriage, would Jack's hardened
heart need protection...from Jillian, his glass slipper bride?

September 1999 MARRIED TO THE SHEIK
Carol Grace (SR #1391)
Assistant Emily Claybourne secretly loved her boss, and now Sheik
Ben Ali had finally asked her to marry him! But Ben was only
interested in a temporary union...until Emily started showing him
the joys of marriage—and love....

November 1999 THE PRINCESS AND THE COWBOY
Martha Shields (SR #1403)
When runaway Princess Josephene Francoeur needed a
short-term husband, cowboy Buck Buchanan was the perfect
choice. But to wed him, Josephene had to tell a *few* white lies,
which worked...until "Josie Freeheart" realized she wanted
to love her rugged cowboy groom forever!

Available at your favorite retail outlet.

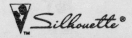

Silhouette®

THE FORTUNES OF TEXAS

This **BRAND-NEW** program includes 12 incredible stories about a wealthy Texas family rocked by scandal and embedded in mystery.

It is based on the tremendously successful *Fortune's Children* continuity.

Membership in this family has its privileges...and its price.

But what a fortune can't buy, a true-bred Texas love is sure to bring!

This exciting program will start in September 1999!

Available at your favorite retail outlet.

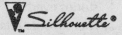

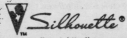